SCREEN TEST

David Klass

SCHOLASTIC PRESS / NEW YORK

Library of Congress Cataloging-in-Publication Data

Klass, David.
Screen test / by David Klass.—1st American ed.
p.   cm.

Summary: While starring in her first feature film, sixteen-year-old Liz
is dazzled by Los Angeles and a charming and handsome leading man
and wonders what it will be like to return to her normal life
in New Jersey.
ISBN 0-590-48592-X (HC)
[1. Motion pictures—Production and direction—Fiction.   2. Actors
and actresses—Fiction.   3. Los Angeles (Calif.)—Fiction.]
I. Title.
PZ7.K67813Sc
[Fic]—dc21   96-48174

10 9 8 7 6 5 4 3 2 1

Printed in the U.S.A.
First edition, October 1997
Design by David Caplan

For Michelle and Paul

CHAPTER 1

People have always told me I was pretty.

When I was two, the owner of the local photography store asked my parents if he could hang one of my pictures in his window display. I'm still hanging there fourteen years later, a little girl wearing a soft pink robe, smiling delightfully out at Broad Avenue. Sometimes when I pass by and the street is empty, I make a face back.

The baby-fat years nearly killed me. My cheeks and chin were nearly pinched off by bony-fingered relatives at family get-togethers.

And then came problems with boys. In the second and third grades, they simply tried to look up my dress and pull my hair and write all over my schoolbooks. But around the end of elementary school, I began to make boys so nervous that they did stupid and dangerous things in my presence. Poor Abner Peck was watching me in coed gym class in seventh grade when a softball hit him in the face and broke his nose. At the town pool the first summer I wore a bikini, Todd Fraser tried to impress me by doing a double flip off the high board and ended up belly flopping and giving himself a hernia.

It's not that I don't like attention from guys. It's just that I often catch them staring at me like I'm some kind of incredibly rare species of bird that they never expected to see flying around northern New Jersey. Either they get glassy-eyed or a kind of hunger shows in their faces. Both types of looks make me a little nervous.

I'm not elegant or voluptuous or sultry or even classically beautiful. A few years ago I thought my legs were too long for my body, and that I would end up gangly and flat-chested. But I got lucky and grew in all the right places, and guys seem to get a charge out of just looking at me.

I've got chestnut hair, which I inherit from my father, bright green eyes from my mother and grandmother, and a trim body which I take some credit for — I do high-impact aerobics at the Y and swim and play tennis. When I first came to Hollywood they said I had a "quality," which seems to be a good, vague word for it. But I'm jumping ahead of my story, and with a story that takes off as quickly as this one, it's probably better to start slow.

My full name is Elizabeth Anne Wheaton and my friends call me Liz.

The night everything started, I went out on the first date of my life with a boy named Eric Bennett, whom I had gotten to know at my part-time job at Center Pizza. It was two weeks after my sixteenth birthday, which might seem a little late for a first date, but it was worth the wait. I had been asked out lots of times before by older and much surer boys with varsity letterman's jackets and fast cars, and I had always found a polite reason to say no.

The real reason was that I was shy. My father blusters and teases a lot, but at heart he's a very gentle and sweet man, and I guess I wanted to meet a boy who was kind of like him. I don't like to be pressured.

Eric was soft-spoken and a little bit shy, which made me feel relaxed. For nearly a month at Center Pizza we said little more than hello and good-bye to each other, but I'd felt him stealing glances at me while we were working, and I'd stolen a few back at him. Soon we began smiling at each other. When he finally got the nerve to suggest going to a movie on a Friday night, I said I'd love to go.

It was late March — windy and uncertain weather, no longer winter but not quite spring.

I had no idea what to wear. I piled about a dozen different outfits on my bed and tried on a mini with black tights. In the end I decided to just be myself, so I put on my most comfortable pair of blue jeans and a green sweater that matched my eyes. Then I sat at my desk pretending to do homework and stealing glances at the clock. Every few minutes I got up and examined myself in the full-length wall mirror. Too casual? Hair look weird? Less makeup?

Eric arrived right at seven, and when I saw that he was wearing blue jeans and a nice flannel shirt with a collar, I knew that we were going to have a relaxed and fun time. He wasn't handsome the way boys are in magazine ads. His neck was too long for his body, and no matter how hard he tried to comb down his thick black hair, it rose tangled and unruly — halfway between a mop and a giant fuzzball. But when he smiled his cheeks dimpled, and I liked the way his gray eyes watched me whenever we were in a room together.

We went to a comedy at the Cineplex and shared a large popcorn. The movie was a little dull, but when our fingers brushed and pulled away in the darkness, I got small electric jolts.

After the movie we went to Jake's Diner for ice cream and talked about our jobs at Center Pizza and school and our summer plans. Eric said his family always took a beach house at the Jersey Shore for the months of June and July.

"There're five bedrooms — tons of space for guests," he assured me, halfway through a vanilla shake. "So if you want to come for a day, or even stay for a couple of days, there wouldn't be any problem with space. I mean, I know the summer's still a long way off, and you probably don't even like the shore, you probably hate the shore, but it would be fun to have you there."

"I've never been to the shore," I told him, picking the chips out of my chocolate-chip ice cream with the tip of my spoon and crunching them between my teeth.

"You mean you've grown up in New Jersey and you've never been to the Jersey Shore?"

"Never."

"Wow."

"Why wow?"

He shook his head. "What do you do in the summer?"

"My parents are both teachers, so they get summers off. We go on trips together. To Mexico, or into Canada, or one summer we went to Europe."

"But never to the Jersey Shore? So you've never been to Seaside or Long Beach Island or Atlantic City?"

"Never."

"Wow," he said again, and watched me eat my ice cream. Gradually his look became a gaze, and then a stare, till suddenly he was watching me so intently that his gray eyes seemed to almost reach out for me.

"What is it?" I asked.

He hesitated for a very long second, and when he finally spoke he blushed a little bit. "When you're smiling — when you get this certain cute look on your face — did anyone ever tell you how pretty you are?"

"A few times," I answered truthfully, feeling uncomfortable.

"They did?"

"Uh-huh."

Eric thought about that. "Well, did anyone ever tell you what a slob you are at eating ice cream?"

I couldn't help grinning. "No, never."

"Watching you pick out the chocolate chips and grind them between your teeth is grossing me out."

"Do they eat ice cream with better manners at the Jersey Shore?"

"They eat lobster at the shore."

"All the time?"

"Come and see for yourself."

"I just might," I told him, crunching the last of the chocolate chips between my teeth.

He walked me home and climbed my front porch steps with me. I live in a big old house, and even with the porch light on there are corners of the porch that are always half hidden in shadow. We were standing in one of those corners now. "Want to come in?" I asked. "My mom'll make you a cup of tea — no charge."

"Thanks, but I should go."

"Oh, well, I'll see you at work on Tuesday."

"Yes."

"I had a really good time, Eric."

"You did?"

"I don't know why, because you're such poor company, but I really did."

"Yeah, well I had a good time even though you're such a slob," he said. "Think we could stand each other's company on another date?"

"I doubt it. But maybe . . ."

"Like next week?"

"That soon, huh?"

"Like maybe next Friday?"

"I'd love to. I'm getting cold. I should go in now."

He stepped closer. "Liz?"

All I saw were his gray eyes in the porch light. Maybe I said yes or maybe I just thought it, and then his head came down and we gave each other a slow, clumsy, and delicious first kiss.

He broke away and stepped back quickly. " 'Night."

" 'Night," I answered.

He stumbled going down my front steps and turned quickly to see if I was still watching. I was, of course, and when I waved we both laughed and he waved back, and then he was gone.

I felt my face — my lips and cheeks seemed warm, almost hot. I waited ten long breaths before I opened the front door and went into my house.

My parents were both in the living room. My dad

was just finishing *The New York Times* crossword puzzle, which he does every night in pen to show the world that he's an intellectual snob. Otherwise he's a pretty nice guy. He teaches American history in a high school in New York, so any puzzle questions having to do with history or current events immediately get nailed. He has a ragged mustache and brown hair that's still thick to the point of being shaggy. When he relaxes in the evening he puffs away on an old pipe and exhales little rings of smoke. I know smoking's bad for your health, but I confess I've always liked the smell of Dad's pipe tobacco and the way his pipe looks drooping from a corner of his mouth.

As I entered the living room, Dad took the pipe out of his mouth and asked, "Do you happen to know a five-letter word for an island south of the Bay of Naples, beginning with a 'C'? It seems to have slipped my mind."

"Corsica?" I suggested. "No, too long. Corfu?"

"The island to which your father is referring is Capri," my mother told me without looking up from her novel. "And he's just teasing me about not remembering it since that's where we had the most romantic honeymoon in the history of the world. Isn't that right, Thomas?"

"I suppose it was a pleasant enough place to spend a week," he admitted, scratching his ear. "They make a rather strong red wine there that I remember fondly. . . ."

My mother put down her book and shook her head. She has the most incredible green eyes, and when she moves her head her brown hair cascades around her shoulders. I always thought she was the true beauty in our family. "He was such a passionate and romantic young man," Mom told me. "How sad that his prime was followed immediately by his dotage." Then she looked at me. "Speaking of passion, how was your big date?"

My father lowered his newspaper and watched me carefully above the headlines.

"Fine," I mumbled.

"Just fine?"

"Fine. Good. Swell."

"Better teach her some more expressive adjectives," my father suggested. Since Mom's an English teacher, he's always trying to blame her for my less than stellar use of the language.

"I've got homework to finish," I told them, eager to avoid further questions. "Good night." I started up the stairs.

"Not so fast, young lady," my father said. "Katy, tell her about her big break."

I stopped, with my foot on the first step. "What?"

"Newton stopped by and asked a strange favor," my mother said, and waited patiently as I rolled my eyes. Newton was the half genius, complete nerd who lived next door. He had graduated from Harvard with almost

9

straight A's. Now he was in graduate school in New York, studying filmmaking, of all things. He was a nice enough guy, but when you asked him a polite question he could go on for fifteen minutes without really answering you. Mostly when I bumped into him on the street I just nodded hello and hurried on by.

"I don't see what you have against him," my dad said. "He's a very nice young man with quite an interesting mind. He's doing very well in film school, and he's decided that he wants to be a director."

"A movie director?" I asked. "Him?"

"Yes. And now, to get his master's degree, he's making a short film — I think it's a comedy — and he wants you to be in it."

At the suggestion that I act in a movie, a cold pang of excitement and fear slithered quickly up my spine so that I shivered. "I don't know enough about acting to be in a movie. Tell Newton thanks, but I'm not interested."

"Why?" my mother asked. "You were so good in all your school plays."

The truth is, I had only joined the drama club and done small roles in a few school plays because my friends Barbara and Amy had joined. I had never taken a single acting class, and I wasn't about to make a fool of myself on film. "I don't want to get involved with one of Newton's projects," I told them, shaking my head. "It'll be an endless hassle. I don't know anything about movie acting. And I bet the part is silly. He probably wants me to dance around in the background in a cheerleader suit or something."

"Actually," my mother said, "the role is for a brilliant young female chess champion, and it sounds like a lot of fun. Newton left the script if you want to take a look. But if you really don't want to do it, I'll call him tomorrow and tell him you're too busy."

She handed me the script. "A brilliant chess champion?" I muttered, thumbing through it.

"Yes, it does seem odd," my father agreed. "I do hope his directing is better than his casting."

I stuck my tongue out at him, said good night to both of them, and headed upstairs.

I read the script through in bed, and I had to admit that it was pretty funny. Several times I found myself laughing out loud. The movie was about a guy who looks for old-fashioned romance and only finds modern superwomen who are so busy with their careers that they have no time for him — kind of a role reversal on the usual story of a nice girl falling for men who are obsessed with money and their jobs.

I was pretty sure, though, that I was dead wrong for the part. Who would believe me as a chess champion? I had never even seen a chess champion — how could I possibly pretend to be one? And what did I know about acting, let alone in a movie, where every expression I made and every bit of bad acting I did would be frozen on film for eternity? No, this was clearly one of Newton's bad ideas, and if I wanted to save myself a lot of embarrassment, I should just politely say no.

I put the script away on the shelf above my bed. Most of my favorite books are there — *Born Free*; *All Things Bright and Beautiful*; *The Black Stallion*, which I practically memorized when I was younger; Jane Goodall's *Through a Window*, about her work with chimpanzees in Africa; and a dozen or so other books about animals. I've done volunteer work in an animal shelter during two summer vacations, and I'll read just about any book if it has something furry in it. The screenplay didn't quite fit next to all of those small and beloved volumes, but I wedged it in and turned off the light.

I'd love to have a real pet, but my father has a terrible allergy to animal hair. So my room is full of exotic stuffed animals, and several of them are piled on top of my thick coverlet. I've got a gazelle and a cheetah, two zebras, and a magnificent lioness with glowing yellow eyes to stand guard in the darkness. I pulled the covers up to my eyes and scrunched down beneath that menagerie of friendly warmth, and thought about my date with Eric.

He had looked so nice in the flannel shirt when he came to pick me up and so cute in the diner when we were teasing each other and so serious when he bent his head to kiss me good night.

I tried to relive the kiss, and I tried to imagine spending a week with him at the Jersey Shore — walking on the sand holding hands, frolicking in the surf — but I finally had to admit to myself that I just wasn't in the right mood. My mind kept wandering away from him.

So after fifteen or twenty minutes I switched on my night lamp, turned on a CD real low so it wouldn't bother my parents, pulled down the script, and read my part through again. This time I whispered my lines and imagined saying them before a camera.

— "Pawn to king five."

— "Would you mind not tapping your finger? The slightest sound disturbs me."

— "I'm not here to *watch* the chess champion. I *am* the chess champion."

— "And that, my friend, is checkmate."

CHAPTER 2

Newton had the silliest pair of eyeglasses I've ever seen. They were thick and round like bottle bottoms, and they looked like they'd gone out of style a century ago. His black hair was already receding from his forehead, and his scalp showed in tiny patches above his ears and on the crown of his skull.

On the weekend of the film shoot he was hopping from place to place so quickly that it almost made me dizzy to watch him. One minute he was telling me to relax. "I saw you in the high school production of *Our Town*, and you were terrific. You're a natural. Just don't tense up on me." The next minute he was on the other side of the room talking to his technical crew about how to set the lights.

The fact is, I was very nervous. It turned out that all the other actors were professionals from New York. Newton had cast an experienced actress in my part, too, but she had gotten a TV soap opera role and left the project at the last minute. I was the best Newton could do as an emergency replacement.

The male lead actor sauntered over and introduced himself as Jeff. He was handsome but slightly dorky-looking — perfect for the part. I felt he lacked enough of a likeable quality, but that might have been because he was apparently miffed at having to act opposite an amateur and wasn't particularly friendly toward me. "Just hit your marks and don't blow your lines," was all the advice he had to offer me.

Newton wasn't much help either. He seemed more concerned with the technical aspects of filmmaking than with my performance. He never talked to me about my character's motivations or about the differences between acting for the stage and for the screen. "What does it mean to hit my marks?" I finally asked him.

"I thought everybody knew that."

"Well, I don't."

"As we set the lights and figure out the camera moves, we'll put down pieces of tape to show you exactly where to stand or move to during the shot. Those pieces of tape are your marks."

"What happens if I miss one?"

"You'll mess up the composition and you may end up out of focus. Just don't tense up and you'll be fine."

I always thought that the process of shooting a

movie would be very exciting. Actually, it was tedious. It took the technical crew more than an hour to set up for the first shot. While they checked and rechecked the focal distances and the lights, we had to walk through our blocking again and again, hitting all the right marks at the right times. I began to wonder if we'd ever get the shot off.

The first take, however, was electric. When the lights were all set and everything had been measured and checked and rechecked, the fat little man who was serving as Newton's assistant director shouted: "QUIET ON THE SET! This is a take!"

I was in my first position, standing by the chess table. I could feel my heart pounding, and swallowed several times to try to overcome my nervousness.

"Camera ready?" the assistant director asked.

"Ready," the cameraman replied.

"Sound ready?"

The young woman holding the boom microphone answered, "Sound ready."

"Roll sound."

The other sound person flipped a few switches on the recorder and shouted, "Rolling."

"Roll camera," the little man said, his voice quickening with excitement.

It was so quiet you could actually hear the film begin going through the camera as the cameraman shouted, "Rolling."

"Mark it."

A member of the technical crew, standing in front of the camera, shouted, "Scene two, shot five, take one," and snapped the top down on a slate that had a lot of chalk writing on it. He jumped back out of the way.

The fat little man glanced at Newton, who was crouching just below the lens of the camera, studying the scene from the exact same angle it would be filmed. "ACTION!" Newton shouted, and his voice quivered.

I pretended to be watching a chess game, and then glanced up and saw the male lead for the first time. We exchanged a quick look. He smiled, and I frowned and went back to watching the game. He walked over and said, "Hi, how's the game look?"

"Fascinating," I responded, all of my interest fixed on the chess pieces.

"Not very many women come to watch chess tournaments."

"I didn't come to watch," I said, feigning irritation.

"You just happened to be passing by and wondered what we were all doing here?"

"No," I told him. "I'm playing in this tournament."

"Well then, why are you watching someone else's game?"

"Because I've already won mine. Please excuse me." I walked away, leaving him staring after me.

"CUT!" Newton shouted. The cameraman took his hand off the trigger.

"How'd it look?"

"Okay," the cameraman said without enthusiasm. "I

17

had trouble keeping her in frame. She's moving her head too much."

"We can only afford one more take," Newton told me. "Try not to move around so much. Opening composition. LET'S GO!"

It was a killer of a weekend. I was very impressed by how hard everyone worked, particularly since they were all apparently volunteering their time on Newton's film. We shot clear through to ten P.M. on Saturday, and on Sunday we didn't wrap till after eleven.

I was totally surprised when Jeff, the male lead, who had been cold and condescending to me all weekend, asked me out after we finished shooting on Sunday night. "You're not bad," he admitted. "With a little training, I think you could hold your own. Why don't you give me your phone number and we'll go out for a drink sometime soon in the city and talk about your acting career?"

"Sorry, I don't have an acting career," I told him.

"What do you want to be?"

"A veterinarian."

"No kidding? We'll, let's go out anyway. I know a great dance club on the East Side."

"Sorry," I told him, "but I'm real busy in school right now."

He looked like he would keep arguing, and then I guess he read in my face that I really wasn't interested in him. He turned and without a word walked away.

"Thanks so much for your help," Newton said as he

drove me home on Sunday night after the shoot. "Everybody says you were just great."

"It was fun. When will the film be finished?"

He shrugged nervously. "Normally it would take months to do the editing and put the sound tracks on and get everything just right. But there's going to be a student film festival in Los Angeles in May, at the Academy of Motion Pictures." For a second his voice dropped and a dreamy look flashed over his face. "Imagine, the Academy Theatre. Nearly two thousand seats, and all of them filled with people from the film industry — agents, producers . . ."

"So you're gonna try to rush to get it finished in time to enter it in that festival?"

"Yup. I'm hiring two assistants to help me, and I've got a volunteer who'll work on the sound tracks just for the experience and a screen credit. With any luck I should be able to finish in time for the festival. As soon as I do, I'll get you a video copy so you can see what we came out with."

He pulled into his driveway and we both got out. "Well, thanks," I said again. "I hope it launches your career."

"I hope so, too," he muttered. "You have no idea how much time and money I've put into this thing already. And it's such a flukey business out there . . . who knows what they're looking for. . . ."

"I'm sure your comedy will do just fine," I told him. "Good luck with the editing. Bye."

"Bye."

I walked over to my house and went in. My parents were in the kitchen, having some tea before bed. "So, here's the big movie star, back from the shoot," my father said. "Tell us about the world of the silver screen."

"Would you mind moving over a few feet?" I asked him. "You're in my light."

Mom and Dad looked at each other. "Thomas, I think she's gone Hollywood," my mom said. Then, to me, "Want a cup of herbal tea before bed?"

"Don't be plebeian," I told her. "Pink champagne, please."

CHAPTER 3

You never know when a day that seems perfectly normal will turn out incredibly weird.

I started by having a nice normal breakfast with my family — cornflakes for Mom and me; eggs and bacon and two cups of coffee for my father, who needs big doses of protein and caffeine to get him started. I walked with my two best friends, Barbara and Amy, to school, and we gossiped about which junior girls had been asked to the senior prom. Barbara and I were perfectly content to just go next year, when we would be seniors, but I could tell that Amy was hoping that a senior would ask her in the next few days.

Homeroom was normal. I finished up a little homework and listened to the announcements about a baseball game and a tennis match after school. First period was about as good as you can expect an early morning chemistry lab to be. Second period history and third period English passed by uneventfully. And then, in fourth period band practice, things started to get strange.

Actually, the band practice itself was pretty standard. I sat in the middle of the flute section, watching Mr. Raucci wave his conductor's baton back and forth with enough energy so that by the time we started rehearsing "Pomp and Circumstance" for the upcoming graduation ceremony, trails of perspiration were parading down his forehead.

The bell to change classes rang halfway through "Pomp and Circumstance," and Mr. Raucci lowered his baton in fury, as if the school routine and the clanging bell were interfering with his attempts to create art. I hurried to put my flute away and was just locking up the case when Brian MacIntyre walked over. He must have put his saxophone away already, and he surprised me by tapping me on the shoulder and saying, "Hi, Liz. How goes it?"

I didn't know Brian that well. He was the captain of the tennis team and played first sax in the band, and he seemed to be a nice, good-looking senior with lots of friends. Sometimes we said hello to each other in the band room or in school hallways, but in three years of band together I don't think we'd ever had a serious conversation. "It's going okay," I said. "How's it going for you?"

"Good," he said. He seemed a little nervous. "We have a big tennis match today."

"I heard the announcement in homeroom. Who's it against?"

"Harrison."

"Will we win?"

"Too close to call."

I succeeded in locking up the flute case and he surprised me by taking it out of my hands and laying it in its place on the rack in the storage closet. "Thanks," I said.

"No problem. Got a minute?"

"I have math next." It was on the other side of the school building.

"I'll walk you." We left the band room and started down the long gray corridor. Rows of four-foot green metal lockers rose from the floor halfway to the ceiling. We walked through a crowd, and Brian made some small talk about how boring band practice always is. As we turned toward the math classrooms the crowd thinned out till we were alone for a minute. Brian slowed and then stopped, and I followed his lead.

"I know this isn't a good time to talk," he said. "You probably have your mind on logarithms and multivariable equations and stuff like that. But . . ." He took a deep breath. "I've been sitting there pretending to play the saxophone and secretly admiring you for a couple of months, and . . ." He actually trembled slightly, caught himself, and forced a smile to his lips. "What I'm trying to say is that I think you're terrific and very beautiful. I'd like to ask you to be my prom date."

I was amazed, and touched by his sincerity. I could tell that it wasn't easy for him to ask me this way. There were at least a dozen girls who would have jumped at the chance to go with him. I couldn't think of why he chose me, and I was surprised that he looked so nervous. "I'm flattered," I said. "I really am."

"I don't want you to be flattered. I just want you to say yes."

I looked back into his black eyes and he read my answer.

"Why not?"

"I'm kind of . . . going out with somebody."

"You are?" Surprise and even a kind of anger showed in his face for a second. "Who? I haven't heard about it."

"He doesn't live in this town. I work with him at Center Pizza. We've just started going out but . . . I can't go to the dance with you. I'm sorry."

"Me, too," he said. We stood there in the empty hallway with him looking down at me with disappointment and desire flashing in his eyes. He took a half step forward. I got the crazy feeling that he was about to put his arms around me and kiss me.

I backed up a step. "I've got to go," I said. "To math, I mean. Mr. Olivera gets angry when we're late."

Brian swallowed. For a second more he looked at me, and I found myself shaking my head very slightly from side to side.

"Then go," he said in a low voice. "Go."

So I went. But all during math class, I couldn't stop thinking about the encounter in the hallway and how strange it seemed for a popular senior who could have gone to the prom with any number of girls to ask someone he barely knew. I could count on my fingers eight or nine nice and very pretty girls he was much friendlier with. So why ask me? The whole equation made as little sense to me as the trigonometry problem Mr. Olivera spent twenty minutes discussing.

My next period was lunch. I usually sit with friends, but the experience with Brian had weirded me out so much that I wanted to be alone. I bought a tuna salad at the cafeteria's food counter and chose a seat at an empty table. I opened up my chemistry textbook and began studying for a quiz we were going to have the next morning. I had to do really well in my science classes to get into a good pre-vet program. But I hadn't been sitting there for more than five minutes when Evan Carlson, a senior guy whom I had known for years because our parents belonged to the same church, sat down next to me. He was the editor of the school newspaper, and he had a nice way of always seeming interested in your business and what you had to say. His sandy blond hair hung almost to his shoulders. "Got a chem test next period?" he asked.

"Tomorrow."

"Then why're you sitting here in isolation studying so hard?"

"No reason."

"Are you feeling okay?"

"It's just been a weird kind of a day," I told him.

"Weird how? Weird bad?"

For a split second I thought of confiding in him, but even though we had known each other for years, he wasn't a close friend. And I figured that what had happened between Brian and me was something I should keep to myself. "Just strange."

"How's the tuna salad? It doesn't looks so great."

"It isn't."

"I saw you talking to Brian in the hallway," he said. "Are you going with him to the prom?"

I guess surprise at his question must have registered clearly on my face. "No," I answered.

"I thought maybe he was asking you."

I stabbed my fork into the half mound of tuna and didn't say anything.

"Well, it's a good thing you're not going with him," Evan said. "Because that means you can go with me."

I caught my breath. "What?"

"I'd like you to come as my date," he said. "We'll have a great time. We'll go with some other couples to a really great Italian restaurant first, and then after the prom there's gonna be a big party. . . ."

"But . . . why are you asking me?" I blurted out.

He seemed confused by my confusion. "Why shouldn't I ask you? You're a girl. I'm a guy."

"We're just family friends. I mean . . . I like you as a

friend but . . . I don't think we've even had a real conversation in years."

"Well, take it from an old friend, you've grown up from the little brat with braces who used to sit behind me in church into a really gorgeous girl. With all that amazing long hair and hourglass figure, you could be in the swimsuit issue of *Sports Illustrated*."

I guess he could tell by the way I was looking at him that he had said something wrong. "Not just that," he added quickly. "I also think we'd have a great time. Look, if you don't want to go with me, just say so. Of course my ego'll be crushed for a month or two, but I'll get over it."

"I'm sorry," I told him. "I'm dating this guy from another town who I work with. I really can't go with you."

He pushed himself up from the table with both hands. "Okay," he said. "We're still friends, right?"

"Yes. Sure."

"Do me a favor. I might want to ask somebody else, so don't let it get around that I asked you first. Okay?"

"I won't tell anyone," I promised him.

I practically ran home from school that day, beset with the ridiculous fear that if I lingered anywhere too long, some guy I barely knew was going to pop out of a hedge and ask me to the prom. An hour or so later when my mother came into my room, I was still nervous and confused. I told her everything that had happened — I know I had promised Evan I wouldn't talk about it, but mothers are exempt from such vows.

"I don't understand what you're getting so upset about," she responded. "It's nice that they asked you. Some girls would love to be getting such attention."

"I know," I said. "At first I did feel flattered. But . . . it's just that . . . they both barely know me. Before today I hadn't exchanged more than three sentences with Brian MacIntyre in my whole life. And Evan . . . he's never sat down next to me in the cafeteria before. We never talk or walk home together or . . . anything. All he could say today was that I'd look good in a bikini in *Sports Illustrated* and I'd make a pretty date for him."

"I guess I understand a little bit of what you're feeling, but just try to take the attention as a compliment," Mom counseled.

"It feels like . . . I've become some sort of trophy. I mean, if they were guys I knew well, I could understand it. But with senior guys I really barely know, the whole thing just makes me feel so weird and awkward."

"Come," Mom said, holding up a videocassette tape. "This should cheer you up. Newton sent it over. It's a working version of that film he made. He said he thought you'd be surprised."

"By what?"

"I don't know. All he said was that he was very happy with your performance. Let's see."

I followed her downstairs and we popped the tape

in the VCR. I guess what Newton must have meant was that I'd be surprised by how much footage of me had ended up in the film. Several of the scenes between Jeff — the star — and the other women had been cut very short, but mine played out real long and with lots of close-ups. I was surprised — make that amazed — to see how long I was on screen and how relaxed and confident I looked.

When the video ended, my mother said, "Well, I can see why he put you in so much. You're the best thing in the movie."

"It's not very good, is it?"

"No, the movie's not so great," she admitted, "and I know that today you're hypersensitive about people telling you that you look beautiful. But" — she wrapped me up in her arms — "I'm your mother and so I can tell you that you're a good actress and you looked great on the screen. And that's a fact."

"I was okay."

"More than okay, sweetheart."

I tried to unwrap her, with little success. "Newton's not gonna get any directing jobs from that," I mumbled. "He should have gone to medical school."

"I think he still might," Mom said. "He just wanted to give filmmaking a try. It was like a dream for him. When you have a dream, it's best to try to follow it, at least for a little while. Try to be a bit more charitable. We can't all be everything we want to be."

"I didn't mean to say anything bad. It's just that . . . you know how he is."

She ejected the tape from the VCR and handed it to me. "You know, you're a very lucky girl."

"Woman," I corrected her.

"Woman, girl, or knucklehead, you're going to get asked to a lot of dances by a lot of men in your life. So you'd better learn to enjoy it."

CHAPTER 4

The phone call came on a bright Saturday morning in May, while I was getting ready to go with Eric to a street carnival.

I happened to be downstairs, and my first thought was that Eric was calling to tell me he wouldn't be able to make it. I darted for the phone, but my father put down his novel and picked up the receiver just a split second before I got there. "Yes?" he said. "Yes, you have the right house."

I could tell by his voice and manner that he was talking to another adult. I felt relieved that it wasn't Eric. I had been looking forward to this date all week. The last few times we had been together had been a little bit strained, and I was hoping we could just have a nice, fun day. I didn't know why Eric had seemed moody lately, but I figured a May afternoon at a carnival would be the perfect medicine for whatever was bothering him.

"I see," Dad said, looking a bit surprised. "Yes, I'm her father." He was listening intently. I mouthed, "Who is it?"

He shook his head at me, listened for a few more seconds, and then suddenly raised his eyebrows dramatically. "We can talk about things like money later on," he said. "If you're just in town for two days, she's busy today but I think she will be free tomorrow afternoon. Would you like to come here, or shall we come to your hotel?"

I was practically jumping up and down with curiosity. "Dad, who is it? If it's for me, you should at least tell me."

Dad gave quick directions to our house, and said, "Shall we say about three, then? Fine. We'll look forward to it. Good-bye." He hung up and gave us one of his "Get ready for this" looks. "That was someone calling about you, Liz."

"I gathered. Who was it? Why didn't you let me talk to them?"

"Because I know how sometimes you turn things down very quickly, and this sounded like an interesting opportunity."

"You should have let me talk. The call was for me. I'm not ten years old anymore."

He thought that over, and nodded. "I apologize," he said. "You're right, I should have let you handle it yourself. But I didn't want you to turn down this opportunity sight unseen. I figure you'll get a chance to do that tomorrow, when you meet this man in person."

By the time Eric came to the door about thirty minutes later, all thoughts of the carnival had vanished from my mind. I guess he picked up my vibes, because we had a mostly silent bus trip to Fort Lee, and even a ride on a gravity-defying roller coaster called "The Spin Cycle" didn't shake me into my usual happy-go-lucky state. Eric wasn't exactly a barrel of laughs either — whatever had been bothering him for the last week or so was obviously still on his mind.

"So," he finally said as we took time off from the rides to walk a little bit away from the crowd and eat some cotton candy. "What's with the gloom?"

"Nothing, really. I'm sorry."

"Did six more senior guys whom you barely know invite you to the prom?"

I was glad he said it and that now it was out in the open — at least now I understood why he had been so moody around me the last few times we'd seen each other. "No. Eric, you really have no reason to be jealous."

"I have a lot of reasons to feel jealous. Guys are always staring at you. Even today, at this carnival."

"That's not my fault. I can't tell every guy on the planet how to behave."

"Maybe not, but how do you expect me to feel

when you tell me that a bunch of senior guys asked you to your prom on the same day?"

"Not a bunch. Just two. And the only reason I told you is because you asked why I was upset."

"It's an important question when you're going out with someone you care about." He was silent for a moment. I nodded — I couldn't argue with that. "Liz," he asked, "why are you upset this time?"

"I'm sorry. I was hoping we could have a fun day. Something happened that has me feeling confused."

"About me?"

"No."

"School?"

"No."

"Your parents?"

"No."

The gray eyes looked perplexed. "Animal, vegetable, or mineral?"

"Celluloid."

"What?"

"Do you really want to know?"

"How can I know if I really want to know until I know?"

That made me smile a little bit. And he smiled a little bit back. "Okay," I said. "I'll tell you. But it's probably nothing. Do you remember I told you about that film I made with my neighbor Newton?"

"The one about the chess champion?"

"Right. Well, I did pretty well in it."

"That doesn't seem like a reason to be upset."

"Newton showed it at some big screening in Los Angeles last week and he sent video copies to a number of agents and producers. And one of them called up today — they're in New York on business and they want to meet me."

The music from the carnival behind us made the ensuing pause seem slightly surreal. Eric stared at me like he didn't quite believe what he was hearing. "You had a bit part in a short student film and now Hollywood agents want to meet you?"

"They're producers."

"Oh, not agents but Hollywood producers," he repeated. "And what do these producers want?"

"They want to talk to me about being in some movie they're making this summer in southern California."

"Oh," he said. He put his hands in his pockets and half turned away. "Well . . . that's great. Congratulations."

I grabbed his right arm and tried to turn him back to face me. "You wanted to know what I've been thinking about, so I told you. Now, tell me what you're thinking?"

"That I'm gonna end up like that small-town policeman who married Marilyn Monroe when she was still a teenager," he muttered. And then he looked at me and tried to joke his way through. "I'll go through middle age pointing out your face on movie posters to anyone who'll listen to me and saying, 'I knew her. I dated her when she was nobody. We both worked in this pizza joint in north Jersey.' And they'll laugh and say, 'Sure, buddy. Tell us another one.'"

An afternoon breeze swirled the knee-length grass around us. We stood there, all alone together, and listened to the carnival music and the distant shrieks of little kids on the roller coaster. "Eric, I didn't even invite these two producers. My father did. He says I should at least talk to them and find out what kind of opportunity this is before I turn it down. I've thought about it, and I've decided that he's right. It can't hurt to meet them."

"I'm sure your father wants what's best for you."

"I don't think he wants his daughter to have a life like Marilyn Monroe's."

"The thing is, I like you, and I'd be sorry if you suddenly disappeared."

"I don't even know if they really want me. Even if they do and I decide to go, it'll just be for the summer."

"I guess I was hoping you'd come down to the Jersey Shore."

I ran my right hand through his unruly mop of thick black hair and ended up tracing a finger down the smooth curve of his cheek. "Don't count me out of that lobster dinner yet."

After that conversation, we walked back and tried to have a good time at the carnival. Eric's not super-athletic, but he managed to knock down a pyramid of milk bottles and win me a big stuffed white panda with cobalt-blue eyes. I wasted three dollars in quarters tossing them onto glass saucers — I don't believe anyone in the history of the world has ever won at that game.

We took a ride through a "House of Horror," where ghouls and goblins came flying out of thick darkness to swoop and howl around our heads. I know it's silly, but rides like that spook me. I pressed myself against his shoulder and he laughed. "Chicken."

"What makes you think I'm afraid?"

"You're shaking."

A ghoul howled close by, and I pressed myself even tighter. "Maybe I'm cold."

"It's ninety degrees in here."

A hairy giant rubber bat connected to invisible threads suddenly fell on my shoulder. I screamed and brushed it off.

"I think you pierced my eardrums with that yell."

"Are we almost out yet?"

"If you'd open your eyes you could see for yourself."

"Just tell me. We must be almost finished."

"Hey, take a look at that slimy monster in front of us. It's looking right at you."

"If there's any monster in front of us, I'm sure it's just a part of this stupid ride."

"It looks pretty real."

"Stop it."

"All teeth and hair and ooze."

"Eric."

"It's about to lick you with its tongue."

"ERIC!" I opened my eyes and we were out of the dark tunnel, back in the late afternoon sunlight. "Thanks for protecting me," I told him. "You sure made me feel safe."

"How about a ride on the Ferris wheel before we go?"

"Will there be any monsters with slime and ooze?"

"No. Unless you think I'm slimy or oozy."

"Definitely not slimy," I said with a grin. "Maybe just a little oozy. But let's go."

We got in a Ferris wheel car and soon we were high above Fort Lee, looking down the backside of the Palisades cliffs at the towns of Leonia, Bogota, and Hackensack. They stopped the wheel for about ten minutes right when we were on top. The light was falling, and the ground seemed very far below us. With the music and the view and the sunset, it was kind of romantic.

"I'm sorry we fought," I told him.

"We didn't really."

Suddenly I wanted very badly for him to put his arm around me. "I'm cold."

"Afraid again, like in the 'House of Horror'? I didn't know you were scared of heights?"

"I'm not. This time I'm really cold."

"Do you want me to lend you my jacket?"

"No."

"It's okay. Here, I think I can get it off. . . ."

I was too shy to tell him, so I leaned against him and he finally got the message and put his arm around me.

"It's a nice sunset," I whispered.

"Average."

"I mean, look at the colors."

"The smog on the clouds makes the colors look that way."

"How romantic."

I leaned my head against his chest. The Ferris wheel car shook very slightly in the afternoon breeze. He looked into my eyes. "Liz?"

"Yes?"

"Can I kiss you?"

"You don't have to ask. We've been going out for almost two months."

He took my hand and kissed me on the lips. I squeezed his hand, shut my eyes, and kissed him back. Just when we both relaxed a little bit and started to enjoy it, he whispered, "Sometimes I wish you were less pretty."

I pulled away and opened my eyes. "What?"

He pulled back also, shrugged, and looked away, out over the view of suburban towns linked by main streets and four-lane highways. "Nothing. Just that I know I'm an average-looking high school guy who's not a superjock or anything. I mean, I work in a pizza joint and play the French horn. And people look at us and they say, 'What's she doing with him?'"

"You don't really think about yourself that way?"

"It doesn't matter whether I think it. It's true. I mean, I don't have a complex or anything. But things would sure be easier for us if you weren't getting asked out by other guys and invited to Hollywood and all."

"How ugly would you like me to be?"

Seconds passed. We looked into each other's faces. Neither of us could think of anything to say. "My brass band at school is gonna give a concert next week," he finally mumbled.

"Would you like me to come?"

"Sure. If you want to."

"Of course I do."

"Good."

"Just let me know what day and time."

And then the Ferris wheel started moving again, and without him putting his arm around me again, or holding my hand, or kissing me, we were soon on the ground.

CHAPTER 5

I'm sure it was the first limousine to ever pull into our driveway.

Dad spotted it, put down his newspaper, and walked to the window. Mom and I ran to join him there, and we all stood side by side, gaping at it. It was new and black and shiny, and about twenty feet long. The driver got out first and hurried around to the passenger side to open the door and hold it.

Two men emerged. The first was very tall, had thick glasses, and was wearing a black overcoat that reached from his Adam's apple to his ankles and made him look a little bit like a myopic Count Dracula. The second man was shorter and stouter, and dressed in an expensive-looking dark suit. The two of them looked around curiously, as if they had never seen a suburban street before. I could see them pointing and making comments to each other. And then they headed up the walk toward the house.

Dad opened the door and greeted them on the porch. He escorted them into the house and introductions were made. The tall one was named Harold and he was the vice president of something called El Toro Productions. The shorter man was named Arvy, and he was the president.

"Charmed," Arvy said to my mother, giving her hand a quick shake. "Such a lovely house you have here. Everything so nice. And such a clean, well-tended street."

"And the town," Harold said in a low voice, as if cuing him.

"Oh, yes, it's a sleepy little gem. Who would guess it's so close to New York? The perfect place to raise a child . . ." And he turned his gaze to me and smiled admiringly. "But then, no longer a child. A young woman. And, if I may say so, quite an accomplished actress. Do you prefer Elizabeth or Lizzy or Beth?"

"My friends call me Liz."

"Okay, Liz it is," he said with enthusiasm, following my father into the living room. "Let me tell you something, Liz. Now don't let this go to your head — but when you first came on the screen at the Academy of Motion Pictures, it was like one big shiver ran through the crowd."

"When he says we shivered, he means we shivered with admiration," Harold chimed in.

"Yes. Admiration. Recognition of beauty and talent. And that unfathomable, undefinable thing in

Hollywood we call . . ." He glanced quickly at Harold, who spread his hands out to either side as if to say, "Don't ask me to name an unfathomable, undefinable thing." Arvy nodded, smiled, and continued in the same smooth voice, "Well, there is no one word for it. It's . . . the thing. A quality. The silver screen loves certain faces, and certain faces light up the screen. And there you were, glittering like a diamond in the rough, stuck in with a bunch of silly NYU and USC and UCLA student films. But we saw it, didn't we, Harold?"

"From the third row, center."

"And I said, even before the lights came on, I said, 'We're going to track that one down. We're going to discover where she's hiding. Because have I got a role for her.' And we showed a tape of your little film to the director of our next movie, Jason Niles, and he agreed one hundred percent that you'd be perfect."

Somehow during Arvy's long speech we had all ended up sitting down in the living room. They were both on the couch. Dad was in his armchair. Mom was on the loveseat. I was in a wooden rocker. I felt kind of dizzy listening to them, but when Arvy finished talking he looked at me like I should say something in reply. "It's very kind of you to say such nice things about me," I told them, "but I'm really not an actress. I mean, I haven't really studied. . . ."

"Acting is a gift from God," Harold said. "Those who are born with it don't need to study too much."

My father took his pipe out of his mouth. "What Liz is trying to say, I think, is that she doesn't see herself as a professional Hollywood actress. She sees herself as a New Jersey high school student. With friends. And a family. And a boyfriend. And things to do here. Is that right, Liz?"

I nodded.

"And even though you two are so nice and so flattering, I think she has her doubts about leaving a life that she's pretty happy with for all the uncertainties of a summer in Hollywood."

When Dad finished talking there were a few seconds of silence. Then Arvy surprised me by starting to clap his hands together, over and over. After four or five claps, Harold joined his boss in giving applause. "Now that was a touching, beautiful speech," the president of El Toro Productions said, slowly standing. "The speech of a father sheltering and protecting his beloved daughter. Am I right, Harold?"

"Very moving," Harold agreed. "Very."

Arvy began pacing around our living room, occasionally throwing me little smiles. "The thing is, my child, we're not going to force you away from your family and friends. We're not here to change your happy life. We came here to enhance it. To offer you an opportunity that I think . . . that I know . . . thousands . . . make that millions . . . of American girls . . . young women . . . would cherish."

"Exactly what opportunity are you offering me?" I asked him.

"We have a film called *Beach Getaway* that will start shooting in June. A warm, family film. A funny, touching, endearing film. It'll be a five-week shoot. In and around Los Angeles. Of course with a highly professional cast and crew. Two-million-dollar budget. Limited theatrical release and then video, and we'll clean up on the overseas market."

Arvy smiled at the thought and began talking just a bit faster. "Here's the story. Two red-blooded American teenagers — an awesomely bitchin' California beach dude and a bookish girl who's just moved to LA from the East Coast — have nothing in common and don't like each other. Just by chance they cut high school on the same day, end up at the same beach, cross paths with a gang of fleeing bank robbers, get taken hostage, and end up falling in love and outsmarting their captors. It's got thrills, chills, romance — a sure hit!"

Arvy took a few breaths, and then finished his presentation: "And now that you know the story, I'm sure you can see why Liz would be perfect for the part. We've seen her act, and our director has seen her act, and we've met her in person and seen how charmingly East Coast she is, how real she is . . . and make no mistake, reality is the only rare commodity in Hollywood, wouldn't you say, Harold?"

"Nearly nonexistent," Harold said, nodding. He

seemed to have withdrawn into the long black overcoat so that only his head and the tips of his fingers showed.

"Madam," Arvy said, turning to my mother, "I would like to offer your daughter one of the lead parts in the film. It's the oldest line in Hollywood, but in this case quite true: I'll make your daughter into a star. Sir" — and he looked at my father — "if she agrees, we'll find some way to house her safely and under supervision for the duration of the film shoot. Liz" — and he looked at me — "Harold was right. God did give you a gift. And now, while you are in the full flower of your young beauty, you should at least give that gift a chance. If you don't like the gold that you find out in them thar hills, you can always come back here."

The more time I spent with Arvy and Harold, the more they made me strangely uncomfortable. They seemed nice, and Arvy was entertaining to listen to, but for some reason I didn't quite believe or trust anything he said. "I don't know," I replied. "I mean, thank you for the offer. I'll have to think about it. And if you have a copy of the screenplay . . ."

Harold produced a bound screenplay of *Beach Getaway* from under his overcoat and put it down gently on our coffee table. Arvy's beeper went off. He took a cellular telephone off his belt, stepped away from us, and spoke a few quick words. I heard him whisper, "Yes, we're just leaving. Yes, yes, we should be out of these godforsaken boondocks in twenty minutes." Then he returned to us and smiled apologetically. "Business, business, business. I'm afraid we have to go now." He took a business card out of a silver holder. "It's been thrilling to meet all of you. I wish we had more time. Numbers for me in New York and Hollywood are on this card."

We walked him to the door, and I was surprised when he took me by the arm and drew me out the door so that as we walked to the limousine I was alone with him for about fifteen seconds. "Yes, you think it over, Liz," he said quickly, in a low voice. "And one more thing. Your salary for five weeks' work would be about thirty thousand dollars."

I almost fell over, but he held me up and continued whispering in my ear. "Now you have nice hardworking parents, and they're obviously proud people so I didn't want to bring this up in front of them. But you know, college is expensive these days. And I'm sure you're planning to go somewhere good, right?"

"Well, if I get in . . ."

"One summer of acting, five weeks' work, could save them from using up their savings for your college tuition. Now, that's something to think about, too." My father caught up to us, and Arvy abruptly broke off to extend his right hand. "Sir, thank you for your hospitality and for hearing us out. It was a pleasure. A real pleasure, sir. May I say a profound pleasure." He pumped my father's hand several times, got into the door that the driver held open, and soon the big shiny black limo rolled off down the block.

My father and I stood side by side, watching till the limousine disappeared around a corner. "Sometimes you meet people and you wonder what strange planet they come from," Dad muttered. " 'Cause those two are definitely not from our solar system. What did he want when he talked to you alone?"

I was quiet for a few seconds. It's true, Dad doesn't make a lot of money. And it's also true that in his own way he's a very proud man. "Oh, nothing." I shrugged. "He was just saying good-bye."

CHAPTER 6

Big decisions come down to small moments.

After countless hours of phone conversations with Amy and Barbara, long talks with my parents and with Eric, and more than a few sleepless nights, I decided to go for it. I made the decision when I was all alone, in the middle of a sleepless night, staring at the moon outside my window.

I can't say what the decisive factor was, but I can still remember the silence of that particular spring night. Occasionally the wind outside picked up and I could hear it gust through the trees, and then there would come a few faint creaking sounds as our old house shifted slightly. The moon was almost full — it dangled between dark smudges of cloud like an old pocket watch, ticking away the seconds. And I lay there, wide-awake, thinking.

I thought about the sixteen years I had spent growing up in this same town, and how a complete change would be real scary, but might also be interesting. I thought about acting, and wondered if Arvy was right and I really did have some God-given talent. It was hard for me to believe, but maybe I really did need to at least give it a try. Most of all I thought about what Arvy had said about saving my parents all that money in college tuition.

The big May moon looked back at me. I took a deep breath and let it out. And then I found myself nodding, and I knew that for better or worse, I had made my choice.

Barbara and Amy thought it was a great decision. They were sorry I wouldn't be around for the summer, but they were full of teasing suggestions about the great times I'd have in the wild world of Hollywood. "Make sure you get your own trailer," Barbara said. "I've read a lot about movie stars, and they all get their own trailers. It's gotta have red and blue stars on the side, and your name in giant letters."

"Forget the trailer; I'm going to give you a camera so that you can take photos of all the famous people you meet," Amy said. "Mostly guys, please. And if any of them ever pass through New Jersey, send them my way."

My parents weren't completely happy with my decision, but I think they knew it was coming. I heard them talking in their own room, in whispers, and guessed that they were more worried for me than they were letting on.

I went for a long walk with Eric and tried to explain my reasoning to him. He was very polite and supportive, but I could tell he was hurt. His gray eyes looked so sad, I felt tears welling up in my own eyes. "So, are you still coming to my concert?" he finally asked.

"I wouldn't miss it for the world," I told him. And two nights later I found myself in a big old high school gymnasium, sitting in an uncomfortable wooden chair that felt like it had been designed by a medieval torturer, listening and watching the Swamp Swingers Brass Band let it all hang out.

There was Eric and his French horn; a saxophonist who squinted at his sheet music as if he was having trouble with his contact lenses; a guy with bad acne who appeared to be losing a wrestling match with a trombone; and a trumpet player who kept trying to catch my eye. I was sitting in the second row, which wasn't such an achievement considering that only about forty people had shown up for the concert. Most of them looked to be family or friends of the performers.

Eric played with great concentration. He never waved or even looked directly at me, as if making eye contact with someone in the audience wouldn't be professional. So after a while I stopped watching him and just tried to enjoy the music. I don't know a lot about brass band music, but I could tell this particular group was uneven. Eric and the trumpet player sounded real good. The saxophone squeaked several times, and the trombone player produced some sounds that sounded like they should come from bathroom pipes.

When the concert was over, I waited outside the school band room with Eric's family for him to emerge. They were nice, friendly people except that they kept peppering me with questions about Hollywood. Eric's little sister Tammy was the worst: When was I leaving? What kind of a film would it be? Would I get to meet any stars?

Finally Eric came out, having shed his brass band outfit. He was wearing jeans and a sweater, and holding his French horn in a case. He thanked his parents for coming, listened politely while they told him how great he was, and then gave them the horn to take home in their car. "I'll be home real soon," he promised. "I just need to walk Liz to the bus stop."

"You're welcome to stay for dinner, Elizabeth," Eric's mother said.

"Thank you, I'd love to. But I really can't today."

"SHE'S GOT TO GET READY FOR HOLLY-WOOD!" Tammy screamed in the crowded hallway, making me feel really uncomfortable. Heads turned. "It's true. She's going to be a Hollywood star," Tammy told them.

Eric's mother took her arm. "Come, Tam. Let's go."

"She's going to be in movies and on TV!" Tammy continued to explain to anyone who would listen as Eric's mother hustled her away. "And she's not going to have to bother with a rinky-dink town like this. . . ."

Her mother yanked her around a corner and her voice gradually faded. "Your little sister's really something," I told Eric. "Listen, I thought your concert was terrific."

"You enjoyed it?"

"You were great and the trumpet player is good, too. Don't look so doubtful. I had a really great time."

We left his high school through the front entrance and headed for the nearby bus stop. "I don't know what Gus was doing, but he wasn't playing music," Eric muttered.

"Is Gus the trombone player?"

"He's supposed to be a trombone player."

"Well, maybe he was nervous."

"You really thought the concert sounded okay?"

"Better than okay," I told him. We were nearing the bus stop. "I enjoyed every moment of it. At least until your little sister started screaming about me in the halls."

"She's a movie addict. She's thrilled that you decided to go. She thinks she's gonna know a star."

I opened my purse and took out a small piece of stationery. "This is my Aunt Peg's address in Santa Monica. I'm going to be staying with her."

He glanced at the neat blue writing and then folded the paper up carefully and put it in his pocket. "You never mentioned that you had an aunt out there."

"She's not a real aunt. She and my mother were college roommates. They've been friends for twenty years.

I haven't seen her in like . . . six or seven years, since she got divorced and left New York and the East Coast."

"And she's putting you up for the whole summer?"

"Uh-huh. My mom called her to tell her about my movie deal, and she said she has a spare bedroom and absolutely insisted that I stay with her. I guess that's what old friends are for."

"I guess so," he said. We reached the bench. He smiled at me, and a streetlight overhead made his gray eyes sparkle. "Well, it sounds like you're going to have a great summer."

"You, too. At the Jersey Shore and everything. I want you to have a good time."

"What does that mean?"

"What do you mean, what does it mean?"

He asked in a low voice, "Do you mean you want me to go out with other girls?"

"I didn't say that. Why would I say that?"

"Well, are you going to go out with other guys?"

"Do you want to go out with other girls?"

A bus swam into view through the darkness, maybe a half mile away. We both glanced at it and then back at each other. "I'll miss this one," I said. "I'll take the next one."

"No, get on it. The next one's not for half an hour, and we both need to get home."

"But we need to talk."

"What is there to talk about?" he whispered. He stepped closer, took my hands, and looked right into my eyes. "You have a great summer. Enjoy yourself. I'll try to enjoy myself. And we'll see what happens in September. If you come back."

"I'll come back."

"Okay, then."

The bus was maybe fifty feet away. He bent his head and kissed me once, quickly, on the cheek. "And try to make a damn good movie," he whispered in my ear.

The bus stopped. The doors opened. "Will you write?" I asked him.

"Sure. You should go now."

"Okay. Good-bye. You will write?"

"She's coming," Eric called to the bus driver, and propelled me up the steps with a gentle push.

I pulled myself up, the doors closed behind me, and even as I was taking out some money the bus started to move. By the time I sat down, we were fifty feet from the bus stop. I looked back and caught one quick glimpse of Eric, his back turned, already starting to walk home. The bus sped away, and he was soon swallowed up in the darkness.

I was almost the only passenger on the bus. I sat there, looking out the window, wondering if I was making a mistake. It would have been great to spend the summer with Eric and my friends, and to take a trip to the Jersey Shore. Instead, I was going to Los

Angeles to live with a woman I barely remembered and to work at a profession I really didn't know anything about, at the invitation of two producers I didn't like or trust. Sitting there on the bus gliding through the silent and empty New Jersey streets, the whole proposition sounded absurd. No, make that insane.

When I got home, my mom showed me a "measurement card" that had arrived by special messenger. An attached note explained that the information would be used by the film's costume designer to start getting clothes for me, and that I should fill it out immediately and fax it back to Hollywood.

After a mostly silent dinner, my mom brought her sewing kit into my bedroom and took out the tape measure. It only took her a few minutes to get all the necessary measurements and write them down one by one on the white card. "Finished," she announced, closing her kit and holding up the card for my inspection. "At least your clothes should fit."

"Thanks." I sat down on my bed.

She looked down at me. "What's wrong, baby?"

"Nothing."

"Nervous about the trip?"

"No, nothing, really, I'm okay." I felt a few tears in the corners of my eyes and tried to blink them away.

She sat down next to me and gave me a kiss on the forehead. "Sad to leave Eric?"

"Kinda."

"Well, we're all sad to lose you for the summer. I'm sure he is, too. But can I tell you something?"

I nodded.

"I think you made the right decision," my mother told me. "Life is to be lived. At your age, when you're offered such an adventure — such a chance to see a new and exciting world — you have to at least try it."

"Yeah, I know," I mumbled. "But don't I at least get to feel a little miserable about leaving?"

Mom smiled. "I feel miserable to see you go. And I'm a little afraid for you. But painful and scary as it is for both of us, that's the way we grow. Your Aunt Peg will take good care of you. She might seem a little bit eccentric at first, but I've known her for twenty years and she has a heart of pure gold. Okay?"

"Okay. But suppose I'm not good at acting? They're paying me thirty thousand dollars based on one short student film. Suppose I fail? Suppose I'm a complete flop?"

She gave me a hug. "Then you can come back here and try to put up with your old parents for another year before college."

I managed some kind of smile. "You won't rent out my bedroom right away?"

"No, not right away," Mom reassured me, using a tissue to dab the wetness from the corners of my eyes. "We'll keep it open for you, at least till the end of the summer."

CHAPTER 7

My plane landed at Los Angeles Airport at five-thirty in the afternoon. There were a dozen or so people waiting at the entry gate to greet passengers from our flight, but Aunt Peg wasn't among them. I waited ten minutes for her, and then went downstairs and retrieved my two suitcases from the luggage carousel. There were no other flights coming in, so the enormous baggage-claim room emptied out. I sat down on a plastic chair and waited.

Here and there, unclaimed suitcases from previous flights stood all alone, or were piled into small pyramids. It's hard to imagine a much lonelier place than an empty baggage-claim room. A janitor pushed a big broom back and forth across the floor and threw me occasional glances. "Are you okay?" he finally asked.

"Yes, thank you. I'm just waiting for someone."

"Sure they're coming?"

"Yes. Thank you. I'm sure." I hope I sounded more

sure than I was beginning to feel. Minutes crawled by. I was just about to look for a telephone to call to see if anything was wrong when Aunt Peg walked through the electric double doors and spread her arms wide. I recognized her from old memories and from a photograph my mother had shown me. She was a slender, youthful-looking woman in her early forties wearing red sneakers, black tights, a black leather skirt, and a red skintight top. "Elizabeth, welcome to California!" Before I knew what was happening she had swept me off the floor in a big hug.

"Is everything okay?" I asked when she set me down.

"What do you mean?"

"I was afraid maybe you'd gotten into a car accident or something . . . and that's why you were late."

"Oh, no," she said. "I'm early."

"My plane got in more than fifty minutes ago."

"I had to give you time to taxi in, deboard, get your luggage — all that sort of icky stuff," she said. "Normally I pick people up an hour after they arrive. But since you're an extra special guest, I made an exception and came early. Now" — she grabbed the smaller of my suitcases and hoisted it up — "you take the other one, and let's get out of this spooky terminal. I don't like airports — unless I'm the one taking the trip."

A few minutes later we were in her Firebird convertible, following a succession of local roads toward the sinking California sun. "You know what the freeways are like at this time of day?" she asked. "Terminal wards. You go in, you might never come out. You're putting your life in the hands of the angry random god of traffic. So we'll just take a few shortcuts, and a few long cuts, and we'll be back in Santa Monica in a jiffy. You are so pretty. Did I tell you that? How old are you now?"

"Sixteen," I managed to squeeze in.

"You remind me of your mother when I first met her. I was so jealous of how gorgeous she was. I always thought she would end up a Hollywood star. And here you are, all set to be in your first movie."

She paused for breath and I asked very quickly, "What do you do, Aunt Peg?"

"What do I do? There's the Pacific, by the way. See? Waving through that gap in the buildings like a little blue handkerchief. Isn't it beautiful? What do I do? Oh, and look, that's one of the best Thai restaurants on the Westside. Do you like Thai food?"

"I haven't really ever tried it."

"What? Never? Well then, that's what we'll eat tonight. We're gonna have a good time together. What do I do? Oh, and this I absolutely have to show you. See that building? That's Gold's Gym. The biggest, strongest, handsomest weight lifters in the whole world pump iron there. We'll go inside another day. Right now we have to get you home and unpacked."

Home turned out to be a very nice and new

condominium on the second floor of a four-story white-stucco building half a mile from the Pacific Ocean. There was a modern kitchen, an enormous living room with couches arranged around a big-screen color TV, and a sunny dining room with a glass-topped table. A short hallway led away from the living room to two bedrooms.

"I hope you'll be very comfortable here," Aunt Peg said, showing me into my bedroom. "No one's ever slept here before. I've been using it for storage. But I cleaned it out this morning, burned some incense to exorcise the evil spirits of dust and mildew, and put fresh sheets on the bed and fresh towels in the bath. There are hangers in the closet, and soap and toilet paper in the cabinet under the sink. Well, it's all yours, Elizabeth. Make yourself at home."

"Okay, Aunt Peg. Thank you. Maybe I'll unpack and take a quick shower. And . . . nobody calls me Elizabeth. My family and friends call me Liz."

"Well then how about we drop the 'Aunt,' " she said. "It makes me feel like I'm some Kansas farm woman in *The Wizard of Oz*. My friends call me Peg. Okay, Liz?"

"Okay, Peg." It felt a little strange to call a woman of my mother's age by her first name.

Thai food turned out to be delicious. We started with chicken coconut soup, and then Pad Thai noodles, shrimp with mint, and mixed vegetables in coconut-milk sauce. Since it was my first time, Peg ordered everything very mild — even so, it was so spicy I could barely eat it. But bowls of white rice helped, and so did delicious sweet iced tea.

"So," Peg said, "you're keen to know what I do, eh? Did your mother tell you what I used to do in New York?"

"I think she mentioned . . . you worked in an investment banking firm?" I said doubtfully.

"For eight years. I was a completely different person then. It was the most stressful job in the world. I carried around two different beepers, and I would put them at the head of my bed when I went to sleep. Sometimes I would work fifteen hours a day for week after week. But I'm glad I did it. I had to get that competitiveness and avarice out of my system. Andrew — that's my ex — was a partner in a big law firm, so with his paycheck added to mine we really lived in style. The only problem was that we never saw each other. I'm not sure we even really knew each other. . . ."

Peg broke off and helped herself to some more shrimp. "It's not too spicy for you, is it?"

"No, it's delicious. Are you and Andrew still in touch?"

"Goodness, no. It wasn't exactly a clean break. Messy, messy, messy. I caught him with another woman. A friend of mine. At sixteen you're old enough to know such things."

"I'm sorry," I said.

"No need to be. Better to know than not to know. Ended the friendship rather suddenly, though. Not to mention my marriage. We sold the brownstone apartment we'd bought together, and he went his way and I went mine. You know the poem, 'East is East and West is West and never the twain shall meet.' With the money I got from the divorce settlement and the sale of the apartment and my own savings, I came out here, bought the place I'm in, invested the rest, and now I do pretty much whatever I want."

"And what is that, Peg?"

We had finished everything on the table. The waitress scooped up the dishes in a big pile and carried them away. "The flavor of the month is flowers," Peg said. "I work part-time in a little shop on Montana. And I do yoga. Also, a lot of volunteer work for battered and homeless women. I've studied French, Spanish, and Italian. I've traveled all over our hemisphere. Taught aerobics . . ."

"It does sound like a completely different life than the one you were leading in New York."

She gave me a little smile. "Are you getting ready to pass judgment on my lifestyle?"

I was surprised by the directness of her question. I guess maybe I had been thinking that her life out here sounded a little strange. I would have to be more careful around Peg — her perceptions were sharp. "No," I said.

"Good, because you're hardly one to talk, Miss Teen Movie Queen," she said, jabbing me teasingly in the arm with a chopstick. "You're a long way from northern New Jersey now. And tomorrow your producers are going to send a car to whisk you to meet your leading man."

"They are?"

"Uh-huh. And do you know who he is?"

"No."

"Tommy Fletcher!" she said like she was dropping a bomb right through the center of our Formica table.

The name sounded familiar, but I couldn't place it. "I still don't know who he is."

Peg threw her hands in the air. "Boy, is this wasted on you," she said with a laugh. "You don't watch the soaps?"

"Not really."

"You don't watch TV movies?"

"Once in a while." I was remembering a face — a face that I vaguely remembered from a few TV movies — and that I think belonged to a name I now remembered hearing some of my TV addict girlfriends swooning over in the cafeteria. "Who is Tommy Fletcher?"

"Oh, nobody much," she said carelessly. "Just the hottest and cutest young star in the universe. So we better get you home for your beauty sleep. Tomorrow could be an interesting day."

CHAPTER 8

From a distance it looked like there was a small battle going on. I saw bright lights and heard gunfire, smelled smoke, and tasted the salty air from the brackish water below.

The scene was being shot on an old bridge in the port area of Long Beach. There were at least fifty people swarming back and forth across the wooden planks on the second level of the bridge — men and women, old and young, camera assistants and bit actors and prop movers and sound engineers, all casually dressed, serious-looking, and carrying different pieces of equipment, from props to light meters to walkie-talkies.

It frightened me that I would soon be the center of attention for such a serious throng. They all seemed to know so much about what they were doing and I was so ignorant about acting and moviemaking.

The young production assistant who had picked me

up at Peg's apartment and driven me to the set marched me right through to the far end of the bridge where the scene was being shot. "This is near the end of the picture," he whispered. "The gangsters find Rob — that's Tommy's character's name — hiding in their van and threaten to shoot him. Come, you can watch the last take and then as soon as they're finished I'll introduce you to Jason, the director."

"I don't want to get in the way," I whispered back.

He threw me a strange look. "Jason will want to meet you," he said. "After all, you're one of his leads. That's him, standing by the camera."

He pointed to a tall, thin man in his mid-thirties wearing jeans, a black T-shirt, and a Chicago Cubs baseball cap. He had a headset on with a little microphone that he could speak into, and he was conferring with a serious-looking man who I guessed was the camera operator. Twice he broke off the conversation to study the blue van parked in front of the camera through what looked like a small black telescope.

"That's a director's viewfinder," my young guide explained. "Helps him see the shot the way it will look through the camera. He's got great visual sense, Jason does. Used to be a director of photography. This is his second picture, and it's going to be a good one."

"QUIET ON THE SET," a big woman in overalls bellowed.

"That's Jane, the assistant director," my guide

whispered very low. "She's terrific, but if she tells you to do something, do it."

"LET'S GET TALENT IN FIRST POSITIONS. I MEAN NOW. IS HE READY IN THE VAN?"

"Ready," someone answered.

The woman in overalls glanced at Jason, who nodded. "ROLL IT," she bellowed.

The shot was slated. A few seconds passed. "Action!" Jason called in a clear, almost musical voice.

Two big men, one wearing a suit and one dressed as a bank guard, got out of the front of the van and walked around to its back door. I knew from reading the script that they were two of the bank robbers. They both pulled out guns. The one who was dressed like a bank guard opened the van's door, and the thug in the suit stuck his head and gun arm half inside and shouted, "Okay, you punk, out of there."

Then he stood back, holding his gun on the open door. Two or three seconds passed. I could feel my heart beating a little faster. And then a young man got out of the van, raised his hands, and faced the gangster. I didn't need anyone to tell me that this was Tommy Fletcher, the rising star. I recognized his face from the TV movies I had seen months ago. Anyway, he had "STAR" written all over him.

First, he was probably the handsomest, most physically perfect human being I had ever seen in my life. Just over six feet in height. An athletic build, but not like a bodybuilder — perfectly proportioned rather than overly muscular. Long, straw-blond hair that hung down to his broad shoulders. Incredible features that would have been pretty if they weren't so masculine. A high forehead. Small nose. Great cheekbones. A cleft chin. And intense powder-blue eyes that looked back at the two gangsters without blinking.

Second, I could tell he was the star by the way he moved. Walking out of the van. Raising his hands. He took his time, and every movement was clean and precise. I can't explain it, but he had a relaxed grace in front of the camera that made you just want to watch him and him alone. He was wearing white sneakers, faded jeans, and a tight T-shirt. "What do you want from me?" he asked the hood in the dark suit.

"Where's your girlfriend?" the hood snapped.

"She's not my girlfriend and I don't know where she is."

"Are you getting smart with me? You think I won't use this?" He cocked the gun and shot twice — blanks, I hoped — over Tommy's head. Tommy winced at the shots. "Next one has your name on it, punk."

There was a moment of silent staring back and forth.

"She got in the other van," Tommy said.

"The hell she did . . ." the gangster growled. "What're you trying to do, play games? You think you can out-smart us? Okay, let's go, down these stairs to the river.

And take a good look at the sky 'cause you might never see it again, punk."

Tommy glanced up at the blue sky and took a deep breath. He managed to look frightened and completely in control at the same time. Then they walked off the set, down a spiral flight of metal stairs, toward the water. Jason let them get completely out of sight before he shouted, "Cut. Nice work."

Jane, the assistant director, apparently interpreted this to mean that they had gotten what he was looking for. "NEXT SETUP," she shouted. "LET'S GO. WE'RE RIGHT ON SCHEDULE."

"Okay," my guide said to me. "It'll take them a while to get the next setup ready. Let's go."

Ten seconds later, I found myself being introduced to Jason Niles. Crew members gave us some room to talk. He recognized my face almost as soon as he saw me and cut the introduction short. "Elizabeth. Welcome." He gave me a long, appraising look, from the tips of my toes to the crown of my head. "So you decided to help us make this movie, eh? Let's hope we can catch those dancing green eyes on film. You're as beautiful in the flesh as you are on tape."

"Thank you," I said, feeling myself blush.

His slight grin became a wide smile. "By God," he said, "I haven't seen an actress blush in ten years in Hollywood. How was your trip out?"

"Fine, sir."

"You can call me Jason."

"My friends call me Liz."

"Well, we're taking a big chance on you, Liz. But I saw your screen test — I guess it was actually a student film — and I was knocked out by it. We all were. Not only are you a natural, but this role was made for you. So we know you can do it."

"I hope so, sir. I mean, Jason."

"I know so." And then he said, "Look at you. You're still blushing. By God. You have a quality, Liz. It just jumps out of you."

I didn't know what he meant, so I stayed quiet.

"You got to see our last take on the van scene?" I nodded. "Be very honest. What did you think?"

"It looked great."

"That's what I like to hear. And Tommy?"

"He's — a great actor."

"And how does he look? Do you think you could pretend to be attracted to him?"

I smiled and nodded.

"Good. Nothing like bad chemistry to screw up a love story. Want to meet him?"

"If he has time now . . ."

Jason looked at me. "Don't be so meek, okay? You're one of the stars of the show. If you want a drink of water, you tell someone and they'll run and get you a drink of water. If a light is shining in your eyes, you tell someone. Got it?"

"I'll try," I said.

"HEY, TOMMY. GIT OVER HERE," Jason called. "And say hello to your leading lady."

Tommy came walking over. The white sneakers rose and fell quietly on the wooden planking. My heart was thumping like a bass drum. What if he didn't like me? What if he could tell how little I knew about acting, or how nervous I was? His sparkling blue eyes took me in from head to toe in a glance, and he smiled as he got close. His complete, easy confidence was reassuring and even a little infectious. I managed to smile back at him.

"What do you like to be called?" he asked.

"Liz."

"Call me Tom. We're gonna have a good time together." He held out his right hand for a shake. His palm was warm, and he seemed to hold on to my hand for just a few seconds more than was normal in a handshake. "Where are you staying out here?"

"With my aunt. In Santa Monica."

"Perfect," he said. "I live in Westwood. Not that far away. You have a great look, Liz."

I didn't know what to say so I kind of mumbled, "I was born with it."

He laughed, and Jason joined him. "Isn't she special?" Jason asked.

"I couldn't ask for more," Tommy said, smiling back at me.

"Well, here's what I want you two to do," Jason said. "The rest of this week we shoot scenes you're not in.

The bank robbery. The car chase. All the stuff in the police station. So while we're doing that, I want you two to spend some time together. Just have fun and get to know each other. Go bowling. Go to the movies. Go . . ."

"I think we can figure out where to go on our own," Tommy told him.

"Yeah, well, you watch yourself," Jason replied, "because this is a sweet, decent girl from small-town America. And I want you to treat her with respect."

Tommy looked at me and raised his eyebrows. "He's afraid we're gonna lose control of ourselves in a sexual kind of a way," he said to me in a loud whisper.

It was an embarrassing thing for him to say, but he said it with such conspiratorial sarcasm that I had to smile.

"Okay, Tommy," Jason said, shaking his head. "That's enough. We need you to get ready for the next setup."

"Boss says I gotta go," Tommy told me. "Great to meet you, Liz. I'm looking forward to spending some time with you, just the two of us, real soon."

"Nice to meet you, Tommy," I said. "You were really good in that scene." Again, the disarming, mischievous smile. As he started to walk away he put his arm lightly around my waist, pulled me close, and whispered in my ear: "If you thought I was good in that one, wait till I get to kiss you." And then he released me and headed off to change his costume.

Jason and I looked at each other. "As the director of this film, I'd better give you some fatherly advice," Jason said. "Do you have a boyfriend back home?"

I nodded.

"Brought his picture?"

"A little one."

"The size isn't important," he told me. "You set that picture up next to your bed. And this week, you go out with Tommy and have a good time with him. He'll treat you well, and with respect. But he's a leading man and he has the . . . confidence . . . and the appetite . . . of a leading man. And underneath all of that fake charm is a hell of a lot of real charm. So if you start to forget who you are and where you come from, you look at that picture next to your bed every morning when you wake up and every night before you go to sleep. Okay?"

"Yes, sir. I mean, yes, Jason."

"Okay," he said. "Good. I'm really looking forward to working with you. I have a free evening three days from now, and I want you and Tommy to come up to my place off Coldwater Canyon to run through your scenes. It will give me a chance to see you act together and to give you some of the basic blocking. Okay?"

"Sure. I'd appreciate as much chance to rehearse with you as possible."

"I'm afraid we won't have nearly as much as either of us would like," Jason said. "But I saw your tape and you have the perfect look, and if you learn your lines beforehand we'll get by okay."

My guide and I began to walk away, but we had only gotten about ten or fifteen feet when a very pretty red-headed girl of about my own age grabbed my arm and yanked me to one side. "Don't even think about it," she snarled in my ear.

"What?" I asked. My guide was hanging back — he looked like he didn't know what to do, so he was letting the two of us talk alone.

"I'll scratch your eyes out, you bitch," she hissed.

No one had ever said such a thing to me before, in my entire life. "I don't know what you're talking about."

Her grip tightened on my arm. "I'm his girlfriend."

"Tommy's?"

"And I'm telling you now, don't even think about it or you'll be sorry."

"I don't even know him. I mean, I just met him for the first time."

"I saw you just meet him. I saw the way you were looking at him."

"Teri, you shouldn't be here," my guide said very cautiously. "Jason told you not to . . ."

"Mind your own business," she snapped at him. And then she turned back to me. "You might get away with that sweet-little-thing-from-hicksville act everywhere else but you don't fool me for a minute. Remember, I warned you."

Anger came to my rescue in this strange situation. I

yanked my arm free. "I'm from New Jersey, not hicksville, and I have a boyfriend of my own back home, and I just came out here to act in a stupid movie. Now, I don't know you at all, but it sounds like if you have some kind of problem, it's not with me."

She pulled back in surprise and stood there gaping as I turned and walked away. My young guide grinned at me as we moved through the crowd. "Good," he said. "You sure told her off. Now you're starting to act like a leading lady."

CHAPTER 9

When I got home from the movie set, Peg was gone. She had given me my own key, so I let myself in and finished unpacking my suitcases. As Jason had advised, I took out my one photograph of Eric and propped it up next to my bed. It was a very small snapshot; he looked lonely and a little silly sitting there on the large, antique bedside table. I made a mental note to buy a nice frame the first time I saw one.

I lay on the bed and studied the snapshot. It had been taken outdoors, in front of Eric's house. I could tell from the foliage in the background that it was spring. Probably about the time we had gone out on our first date. To the movies. To the diner for ice cream. We had joked around and he had invited me to the Jersey Shore. The memories made me smile and gave me a nice, warm feeling.

And then, as I lay with my eyes half closed, I found

myself thinking about Tommy Fletcher. It was almost as if his face somehow managed to superimpose itself over Eric's in my mind. I tried to peel it away, but it was inextricably stuck there, hooked to my imagination by those piercing blue eyes. The more I tried not to think about him, the more he intruded on my memories of home. I tried to force the image away by recalling the end of my first date with Eric, and the awkward kiss we had exchanged outside my house. But in my mind's eye, all I could see was Tommy sauntering across the plank bridge, wearing faded jeans and a tight T-shirt, his arms swinging at his sides and a relaxed grin on his perfect face.

After a while I climbed out of bed, angry with myself. "Liz, you better stop this." I have a bad habit of talking to myself when I'm all alone, and as I paced up and down the bedroom I started calling myself names. "Dummy. You big dummy!" I came to a stop in front of the bedroom mirror. "You didn't like boys who were attracted to you just because of your looks — remember, you thought those guys who asked you to the prom were creeps. So don't start mooning after some actor just because he gave you a nice smile. It's ridiculous. It's . . ."

"Human nature . . ." Peg said from the door. I jumped nearly a foot off the floor in surprise. "Excuse me," she said with a smile. "I didn't mean to eavesdrop, but your door was open and I was wondering who you were talking with."

"Those are lines from the screenplay," I mumbled. "I was just practicing my dialogue. . . ."

"Oh, I see," Peg said, looking and sounding dubious. "Well, you're a very good actress."

"No, I'm not, but thank you."

"Oh, yes, you are," she said. "You sounded very convincing. Now I see why they paid so much for you to come out here."

It was bad enough to be embarrassed, but it was worse to try to hold on to a lie when I was being made fun of. "Okay," I said. "I confess. I went out to the set and met him and now for some stupid reason I can't get him out of my mind."

She entered my bedroom and looked at me carefully. "What's he like?"

I didn't know what to answer so I opened my mouth and then closed it again.

Peg laughed. "Enough said." She glanced at her watch. "Do you want to come work out with me? I have my step aerobics class at two o'clock. Strenuous physical exercise has been known to relieve high anxiety and reduce . . . shall we say . . . emotional stress."

"Okay," I said. "You convinced me. Let's go."

Aunt Peg belonged to a giant sports club that was kind of like a palace dedicated to keeping in shape. "It's expensive," she said as a valet zoomed away in her car outside the front doors, "but to me it's worth it. I come here at least four times a week to swim or for aerobics, so I figure I get my money's worth."

We walked through the doors and I couldn't believe it was just a sports club. It looked more like the lobby of a grand hotel or the main deck of a cruise ship. There was a beauty parlor, a sportswear boutique, a cafeteria serving health food, a massage parlor, and a sit-down restaurant with a piano bar, all immaculately clean and clearly set up for people who had a lot of cash to spend.

Walking from the front door across the lobby, we passed a dozen or so men and women in their thirties who had been so meticulously groomed for their workouts that they reminded me of poodles at a dog show. Young, shapely women with perfect hair and makeup struck poses in designer tights. Sharp-eyed, aggressive-looking men wore boxer shorts and muscle T-shirts.

There were banks of phones on either side of the lobby, and people were chattering away in loud voices, conducting business. "Sammy," I heard one white-haired man say into a receiver, "I'm gonna give you some good free advice. Are you listening? Before you fire her — talk to your lawyer." He listened for a moment and then made a face. "No, no, Sammy, your problem is you're thinking about her. You have to think about protecting yourself."

A tall woman with stylish designer eyeglasses sat next to him on the leather couch, speaking rapidly into another phone receiver. "You tell him I read it and there's no way we can go out with it," she said. "It's soft and we'll get killed in the coverage. Tell him to do something with the second act — maybe a jeep chase — or a helicopter rescue. Or a helicopter chasing a jeep. And if he tries to pull that high-and-mighty-writer act again, ask him if he wants to go back to teaching freshman English in upstate New York."

We reached the far end of the lobby and got towels and locker keys. "Who are all these people?" I asked Peg as we headed into the women's locker room. "Don't they have jobs during the day?"

She laughed at me. "They're the Westside power elite. Realtors and partners in law firms and movie agents — they do their business wherever they want. Home. Car phones. Restaurants. Or their health club."

"Have you gotten to know them?"

"A few guys have tried to pick me up with really cheesy lines. Other than that . . ." She shrugged. "Los Angeles is a hard city to make new friends in. But it's fun to watch what they all wear, and how they act, and what they talk about."

The second floor was the workout floor. There was a basketball court, a vast weight room, a swimming pool, and two rooms for classes. We were just in time to stretch out before the aerobics class started. The music was rock, with a snappy beat. There were ten women in the class; the instructor was a beautiful Asian woman in violet tights. She looked like she didn't have an ounce of fat anywhere on her body. "Okay, ladies," she said at three minutes after the hour, "let's make it hurt!"

I had taken aerobics classes at the Y back home, but they were low impact compared to this. Peg had been right — all thoughts of Tommy Fletcher were soon driven out of my mind. By the time we were done dancing and jumping and stepping on and off platforms, I was huffing and puffing. The other women, most of whom looked to be ten or fifteen years older than me, were in terrific shape. When the class ended, Peg looked as fresh as a daisy. "You should get more exercise," she told me with a smile.

"If I get any more exercise, I might keel over."

We showered and changed, then sat down at the health bar to sip some frozen fruit drinks. A few middle-aged men at nearby tables kept throwing glances at us. "I feel like I'm in a crossfire of laser beams," Peg said. "Whatever you're doing, try to turn it off."

All the glances made me uncomfortable. "They must be looking at you, not me," I said. "They can't be looking at me . . . they're old enough to be my father or even my grandfather."

Peg finished her drink. "This is a city that feeds on youth and beauty. But you're right, they should be ashamed of themselves. Let's go."

When we got home, it was late afternoon. We picked up the mail — the mailboxes were at the front of the lobby — and we were about to head up the steps

81

when a roar sounded on the street behind us. We both turned at the same time and looked out the double glass doors of the building. Tommy Fletcher drove a big motorcycle right up the front lawn and stopped just in front of the steps. He was wearing the same jeans he had been filming the scene in, but he now wore a black leather jacket over his T-shirt and there was a red kerchief tied over his hair.

He spotted us even before the motorcycle stopped moving, waved, and jumped off.

"That looks like your leading man," Peg said to me.

"It is."

"He's a hunk and a half," she whispered.

"Maybe two hunks," I whispered back as he climbed the stairs and yanked a door open.

"Hey, Lizzy Bird," he said, "I hope you don't mind me cruising by on my way home." He glanced at Aunt Peg. "Let me guess — this is your big sister. She's much too young to be your mother."

"Bless you," Peg said to him. "I'm a friend of her mother's. My name's Peg. I'm a big fan of yours."

"And I just became a big fan of yours, Peg," he said with that easy grin of his, giving her hand a quick shake. "Could I take a little walk with Lizzy Bird?"

"That's up to Lizzy Bird," Peg said, picking up the nickname with a smile. "I'm gonna fly upstairs to our nest now. Nice to meet you, Tommy."

She took the little duffel bag with my workout gear and then she was gone. Tommy and I were alone in the lobby of the building. "She's kinda neat," he said. "Are you ready to go for a ride? I brought you a helmet."

I looked at him, and saw that he was serious. "I can't."

"Why not?"

"Because . . . you told Peg we were just going for a walk."

"She's not your mother."

"No, but . . . I don't think she would like me to go on a motorcycle."

His blue eyes sparkled. "Do you always follow the rules other people make?"

"Usually."

"I almost never do," he said. "So I think we can be good friends. Because, you know, opposites attract. Now, which is your apartment?"

I led him upstairs and in a minute he was very politely asking Peg if he could take me for a ride on his motorcycle. He never asked me if I wanted to go. He just assumed that I did. On one level that made me a little angry, but I have to admit that on another level I found his enthusiasm and complete self-confidence very charming.

"If she wears a helmet and you promise to drive slowly and carefully," Peg told him.

"I'll bring her back to you safe and sound," he promised. "Except . . . we might stop off and eat dinner in Santa Monica."

That was the first I'd heard about dinner. But

somehow everything was quickly arranged without my involvement, and in a few seconds we were downstairs at his bike. He handed me a helmet. "I've never ridden on one of these before," I told him.

"It's easy," he said. "It's like the first time you made love — just hang on and try to enjoy the ride."

I could feel myself blush so hard it felt like my face was on fire. Tommy stared at me like he was seeing something he never expected to see. And then, for just a second, he started to blush also. "You are one sweet girl," he said in a husky whisper. "Here, get on the seat behind me." I got on. "And hold me around the waist." I held him loosely. "Hold me tighter." I held him tighter. "Like you mean it, Liz. I don't want to lose you on the first bump." I held him like I meant it. He looked back at me and smiled. "If you want me to slow down, just give me a squeeze."

We roared away, off the lawn and down the block. Maybe he was really driving more slowly than usual, but it felt very fast and pretty dangerous to me. I held on for dear life, my arms clamped around his waist and my chest pressed tight to his back. The air rushed by my helmet with a whooshing sound. I'm embarrassed to admit it, but it felt a little exciting to be holding him that way — his leather jacket was hanging open and I could feel his stomach muscles with my hands and wrists, and also, when he tensed, the large muscles in his back all the way through his leather jacket.

We were soon at the beach. He parked at the edge of the sand, and I took off my helmet. "You're smiling like you enjoyed the ride," he said. "Not too scary?"

"You seemed like you knew what you were doing."

"Never had an accident. Come on. . . ." We walked across the sand toward the setting sun. It was really a picture-perfect Pacific sunset, right off a postcard. Gulls wheeled in slow circles in the air, the clouds were suffused with a soft purple light, and the beach was mostly empty except for a few couples walking hand in hand and two guys riding surfboards a hundred yards or so offshore. It seemed like the most natural thing in the world when Tommy took my hand in his own, as if to guide me, as we neared the water.

"It's pretty," he said, "huh?"

"Yes."

"I'm glad you could come out tonight. I owe you an apology."

"For what?"

"I heard what happened on the set. Between you and Teri. She had no business blowing up at you that way."

"It's okay."

"No," he said, "it's not okay. I hate jealousy. It's an ugly thing. Acting is what I do for a living. I get cast in a lot of romantic roles. You're a nice girl and you just came here from across the country. We should make you feel welcome. Instead, she threatens you."

"She must really love you."

"She loves being with me," he said. "There's a difference."

We walked further along the beach. One of the surfers stood up on his board and managed a long ride. "That looks like fun," I said. "Can you do that?"

He followed the surfer with his eyes, and shrugged. "I don't mean to brag, but I can do just about anything athletic . . . except ice-skate. Yes, I can do that."

"As well as him?"

"Better."

"Will you teach me?"

"It's harder than it looks," he said. "But yeah, sure, I'll teach you. Now, how about some dinner? There are a couple of classy places right near the beach. You like Italian?"

"Sure. But . . . I mean, we're both in jeans?"

"They don't care what you wear in LA as long as you look good in it and can pay the bill. And we fit both categories."

"I didn't bring much money."

He stopped walking. "I asked, so if you want to go it's my treat. Besides *Beach Getaway* I'm in two national commercials and money is flowing in, so you don't have to feel guilty about letting me pick up the check. But if you don't want to have dinner with me, just say so." His usually playful voice sounded serious. "I mean, listen, Liz, we're supposed to act together but if you

86

don't like me or don't want to hang out with me, that's cool. Just say so. We don't have to be friends to work together, and I won't hold any hard feelings."

A breeze blew his blond hair back from his forehead. The blue eyes sparkled and my hand felt small and warm in his. "I want to have dinner with you," I heard my voice say.

CHAPTER 10

The restaurant was on Ocean Avenue in Santa Monica. It was a classy place, as Tommy had said, with candles on the tables and waiters in jackets and ties, but they didn't seem at all hesitant about seating us at one of the best tables, overlooking the ocean. We ordered, and big portions of delicious food soon began to arrive.

"So, does your boyfriend back home in New Jersey get jealous?" Tommy asked me as we attacked salads and an order of *crostini* — slices of bread with various delicious toppings.

"How did you know I have a boyfriend?"

"Because I assume the guys in New Jersey aren't blind."

I thought about how much it had bothered Eric that guys from my school had asked me to the prom. "Sometimes he does."

"When other guys try to talk to you or ask you out?"

"Yes."

"See, I hate that," Tommy said. "It's only natural that men are going to pay attention to you. You're a very beautiful girl."

"Woman," I corrected him.

"Can we agree on 'babe'?" He grinned, and I couldn't help smiling. Our pastas arrived — I sampled mine and it tasted as good as it smelled. "Well, you're a very beautiful babe and guys are going to be paying you attention for a long time to come," Tommy continued. "And whoever you're going out with has to be confident enough to know that deep down you're loyal and you love him."

"It sounds like you've thought about this."

"Yeah, well, we have kind of the same problem," he told me.

"I bet you have it worse than I do."

"TV exposure does strange things to your life," he said. "So what's this guy in New Jersey's name?"

"Eric."

"What does Eric do?"

"He does . . . the same thing I do. I mean, he's a high school student. We work at the same pizza place."

"Is he a big jock?"

"Not really." In my own mind, I sounded almost defensive. "He plays the French horn."

"I bet Eric wasn't too overjoyed about your coming out to Hollywood."

I shook my head.

"See, I hate that," Tommy told me, winding some fettucini with his fork. "Why can't people be one hundred percent for you? If I was going out with a girl, and she got a big break — like maybe a part in a major feature movie — I would be thrilled for her. Her happiness would be my happiness."

"Eric made it seem like I was . . . deserting him," I said. "To be honest, he made me feel a little guilty."

"That's his shortcoming, not yours," Tommy said. "I mean, picture this. He's sitting there in New Jersey, tooting his French horn and feeling bitter and jealous, and your success is eating away at him. If I were you, Liz, I would think twice about this guy."

"You don't even know him. He's really very nice."

Tommy shrugged. "I know the type."

I felt myself getting annoyed. "There's no such thing as a type of person."

"Sure there is," he said. "The more acting you do, the more you'll see that certain kinds of people behave in very predictable ways. I know Eric and I could play Eric. Want to see?" And suddenly, almost in the blink of an eye, Tommy Fletcher slumped down in his seat and made himself look a little nerdy. He blinked across the table at me shyly. His fingers pressed invisible keys, his cheeks puffed up, and I realized he was pretending to play the French horn. Then he said, in a halting voice: "Liz, I don't think you should go to Hollywood. I think you should stay here with me in New Jersey and make pizza with extra cheese."

Tommy was a great actor. He had playing the French horn down pat, and somehow he managed to look and sound just enough like Eric to make me uncomfortable. I looked down at my plate and wound spaghetti around and around my fork.

Tommy saw my reaction and laughed.

We finished our pasta and I ordered a dessert. Tommy just wanted a coffee. "I need to be careful with sweets," he said. "I have a tendency to put on weight."

"I didn't feel too much flab when I was holding on to you during the motorcycle ride."

"That's 'cause I'm careful," he said. "Not to mention the two hundred sit-ups a day."

I thought of Peg and her killer aerobics class, and I wondered if everyone in Los Angeles was exercise crazy. I would have asked him, but at that moment three girls, who looked like they were sisters, approached our table. The youngest of them was eight or nine, the middle one looked to be twelve, and the older one, who led the way, was about my age. A woman — I took her to be their mother — hung back at a distance. They reached our table and stood there for a moment, exchanging looks and giggles.

Tommy smiled at them. "Hi," he said.

"You're Tommy Fletcher, aren't you?" the oldest sister asked.

"Yes, I am."

"We're from Tulsa. Just tourists here. I'm Martha and this is Jennifer and Kristin. We were eating over there — that's my mom and pop — and Jennifer recognized you from your TV shows. We're all big fans."

"And you're the only TV star we've ever met in real life," Kristin, the littlest one, added shyly.

"I'm glad you came over," Tommy said. "How did three such pretty sisters end up in the same family?"

The two younger girls giggled.

"You're even handsomer in real life than on TV," Martha said. And then she looked at me. "Is this your girlfriend?"

"This is Liz," Tommy said. "She's an actress I'm working with now."

"Two movie stars!" Martha said. "You look so perfect together. If you're not going out, you should be." She paused, remembering something. "My little sister Kristin has a favor to ask of you. Go ahead, Kristin."

"No, you ask him," Kristin said, and turned completely away from us in embarrassment.

Tommy looked from one girl to the other. "Excuse me," he said to me. He climbed out of the booth, walked over to Kristin, and tapped her on the shoulder. "Do you want to take a picture with me?" he asked her with a big smile.

She nodded and waved to her mother, who came hurrying over with a camera. Tommy posed for four pictures, one with his arm around each sister and then one with their mother.

"You're really very kind," the mother said to Tommy

as he put his arm around her for the picture. She sounded just a little breathless. "This is the highlight of our trip. I know my daughters are just thrilled. Thrilled." And she led the three of them away from our table, throwing several backward looks at Tommy.

"That was really kind of you," I said to Tommy.

"I got a kick out of it," he said. "They'll take those pictures home and frame them." And then he looked at me closely. "You weren't jealous at all, were you?"

"No. Of course not. Why would I be?"

"Teri would've threatened to scratch that girl Martha's eyes out. And they were just nice girls from Tulsa."

"If I were your girlfriend, the only one of them I would have been a little jealous of was the mother," I said with a smile. "I think she was secretly your biggest fan of all."

"A sweet lady," Tommy grinned. "C'mon, Lizzy Bird. We had our fun for the evening. Let's go."

He drove me home through the dark streets, quickly but carefully. When we reached my house I thought he might try to kiss me good night, and I was wondering how I could politely decline. I guess I was surprised and a little disappointed when he just walked me to the double glass doors and held one open for me. "G'night," he said.

"Thanks for a fun evening." I stepped inside, and then turned. "Are we going to see each other again, before we go to Jason's house to rehearse our scenes?"

"Absolutely. The thing is, I've got auditions tomorrow and the day after. But how about the day after that? We can spend the whole day together . . . and then drive up to Jason's house that evening? It'll give us a chance to run through the scenes together before we do it for Jason, and we might even be able to work in a little surfing lesson in the morning. If you're free."

"I think I can squeeze you into my busy schedule," I said. "Thanks for the dinner. And . . . you're a real gentleman, Tommy."

"You don't know me well enough yet," he said with the final killer grin of the night, and then he turned and disappeared into the darkness.

CHAPTER 11

I must have done six drafts of the letter. The first one began like this:

Dear Eric,

I hope you're having a great summer. I miss you and think of you a lot. It's a little lonely here, without friends or family. Do you miss me? You haven't written or called yet. But I guess it's only been a few days.

It's because I do think of you so much that I feel I'd better write about a subject that's not easy to bring up. Eric, we never finished that conversation we started at the bus stop about going out with other people during the summer. I really care for you and I know you care for me, but I think we need to be honest with one another, and we shouldn't leave something like that up in the air.

I'm not saying I want to go out with anyone, and I'm not saying I want you to, either, but I think we should agree that if either of us does meet someone who we start to like, we

should be free to get to know them without feeling guilty.
And when I come home after the summer is over, we'll both
see how we feel about . . .

And that was where I got stuck and crumpled my first draft up and tossed it in the trash can.

With each successive draft, I wrote less and less about making a decision to go out with other people and more and more about Los Angeles. The final letter that I put in an envelope addressed to him read like this:

Dear Eric,

How are you? You must be making out like a demon at Center Pizza now that you don't have to split the tips with me. I miss you and think of you often.

Los Angeles is really a strange place. There doesn't seem to be any real city, the way Manhattan is a city with skyscrapers and crowds walking around rubbing shoulders. Instead, LA is a patchwork quilt of neighborhoods, some pretty, some ugly, some safe, some dangerous, connected by highways and boulevards that seem to go on forever. Santa Monica, where I live, is pretty and close to the ocean.

Yesterday my Aunt Peg and I did all the touristy things. She took me to the Mann's Chinese Theater, where dozens of old-time movie stars left footprints and handprints in the concrete, with little messages. I put my hands in the prints of Marilyn Monroe, and stood in the footsteps of Humphrey Bogart, and read the funny messages from the Marx Brothers. It really made me feel strange — like I was almost touching all those famous stars from the past. Most moving of all was putting my palms up against the handprints of Judy Garland — I kept thinking of the way she looked in the ruby slippers in The Wizard of Oz. *Maybe there is some magic left in Hollywood after all.*

I haven't started making the movie yet. I met the director and the crew and my costar, and they all seem nice. So far, all I'm doing is studying the script and worrying about what it will be like to get in front of a camera with all those people watching.

Anyway, that's what I'm doing tonight — studying my lines. My Aunt Peg is out on a date and so I'm home alone, with Bobo, the cat, watching TV and saying the same lines over and over, and trying not to feel too lonely. I hope you're having more fun.

Write to me when you get a chance. I think of you a lot.

I made a few "X" marks for kisses and signed my name under a big "Love." And then I folded the letter in thirds and put it in an envelope, and I was left with the *Beach Getaway* script, the TV, and Bobo, who was rubbing up against my knees and purring.

I realized that I knew no one in Los Angeles besides Peg and Tommy Fletcher. It wasn't just that I didn't have any good friends — I didn't have anyone I could call or go see just to chat with.

I tried telephoning my friends Amy and Barbara, back home in New Jersey, but they were both out for the evening. Thinking about the two of them, and wondering what they were up to, made me feel home-sick. If I were back home, I'd probably be out with the two of them, having lots of fun.

There was a serial killer movie on TV that was too scary to watch alone, so I turned it off and began reading one of the dozens of romance novels that Peg had in her living room. It was called *Love Under the Weeping Willows,* and it was so predictable I almost turned the serial killer movie back on.

My parents rescued me from the boredom with a phone call. Mom was on the upstairs line, Dad the downstairs, so that I got to talk to both of them at the same time. "Hi, sweetheart," Mom said.

"Is this my daughter the Hollywood star?" Dad wanted to know.

"It's me," I told both of them. "Sitting home with Bobo the cat, reading a bad book."

"Where's Aunt Peg?" Mom asked.

"Out on a date. With some guy named Arthur."

"Oh, that's the lawyer," Mom said. "She hates him."

"If she hates him, why does she go out with him?" Dad wanted to know.

"She doesn't hate him enough to stop dating him."

"The mind of women will always remain a mystery to me," my father said. "So how's California, Liz?"

"Pretty good, so far."

"Aunt Peg is taking adequate care of you?"

"She's been very nice."

"Have you met the film people?"

"Yes, they've also been nice."

"Could we please have a slightly more critical and detailed opinion about virtually anything?" Dad requested.

"Okay, I met my costar." I tried to think of some safe things to say that would prevent any unwanted parental speculation. "His name's Tommy Fletcher and he's a very good actor and a nice guy. He's going to take me surfing tomorrow."

"Be careful of sharks," Mom said.

"It's kind of hard to be careful of them while you're out in the water," Dad pointed out. "Unless you happen to see a triangular fin when you're only knee-deep, in which case I would advise heading for shore at full speed."

"I'll keep that in mind," I told them. "Any news on your end?"

Of course there was none. One of the nice things about the Jersey suburbs is that nothing ever really changes. My dad was teaching summer school and my mom said she was planning a trip out to visit me in a few weeks. "I'm leaving the stick-in-the-mud at home."

"Could she possibly be referring to me?" Dad wanted to know.

"It'll be just you, me, and Aunt Peg," Mom told me. "And won't we have a fun time without any men around."

"Stay as long as you like," my father teased her. "Not

that I won't miss you, but we'll get you one of those open-ended tickets so that you can keep extending your trip . . . if you feel like it. I wouldn't want to cut short your vacation."

"That's a good idea," Mom replied. "That way if my talent is recognized and they give me a part in the movie, I can just stay."

"It would take a very discerning director to recognize your talent," Dad told her.

I started laughing then, because they loved each other so much and teased each other constantly, and it was fun to listen to, even long distance from New Jersey to California. They kept it going for another ten minutes or so before we all said good-bye.

After the phone call I read a little bit more of *Love Under the Weeping Willows* and went to bed early. When there was absolutely nothing to do, nowhere to go, and no one to talk to, I figured I might as well take advantage of the opportunity to get a good long sleep. It seemed like I had just dozed off when loud knocking came at the door of my room, and a second later, as I was rubbing the sleep from my eyes, Peg burst in.

"Wake up," she said. "He went and did it. Over a plate of Szechuan shrimp at the Jade Restaurant."

"What? Who?" I had been dreaming about surfboards and sharks, and I was only two-thirds awake.

"Arthur," she said, sitting down on my bed. "Wake up, damn it. I need to talk to someone. When he got down on his knees I almost fainted."

I was still half-asleep. "Did your date lose a contact lens?"

"No, he proposed to me."

That woke me up. "A lawyer got down on his knees and proposed to you in a Chinese restaurant?"

"Can you imagine! He said he was planning to wait till after dinner, but he just couldn't. Everyone broke into applause and they were looking at us. It was terribly embarrassing."

"What did you do?"

"Smiled and waited for them to stop watching me."

"And then what? What did you say to him? Yes or no?"

"I told him I care for him very deeply . . . and I was honored . . . thrilled . . . but that I needed some time to think about it."

"Do you?"

Peg hesitated. She wound her fingers together, intertwining them into a giant knot. "Do me a favor," she said. "Get dressed. Let's go out for coffee or something."

"But it's the middle of the night."

"I can't stay in here. Please."

We drove to a coffee shop that was open late and sat by the window, looking out at the cars streaming east and west on Wilshire Boulevard. "I barely know him," she said. "We've only been dating for . . . a little more than four months."

I thought fleetingly of Eric. We had had less than

three full months together. "That seems like enough time to get to know somebody," I told Peg.

She looked angry for a second, and then shook her head and laughed. "You're just like your mother. Too sensible to be any real help in a crisis."

"All I meant was that if you've been dating him for almost half a year, you must like something about him."

"He treats me with respect," she said. "He has a good job and that confidence that men have when they're successful at what they do. He's smart and nice-enough-looking."

"What don't you like about him?"

"He's . . . a lawyer. I've already been married to one of those and it didn't work."

"That's not really Arthur's fault."

"That he's a lawyer or that I was once married to one and it didn't work out?"

"Both, I guess."

"Whose side are you on?" she asked suspiciously.

"There are probably good and bad lawyers, just like everything else."

"If you say one more sane, sensible thing I might have to empty this cup of coffee on your head." Peg picked up her cup, as if to act on her threat, but she only took a big sip and set it back down. "And you're one to talk, walking around all gaga over some actor-hunk you don't even know."

"I'm not gaga."

"I know gaga when I see gaga. Now, let me tell you something about lawyers and . . . life in general . . . that you might not be aware of but is very true. After a while, you become what you do."

"I'm not sure what you mean."

"Go out with an undertaker and you'll start to feel like a corpse. Date a dancer and you'll have a grand time till the music stops. Bankers obey rules. Writers live in their own dreamworlds. Teachers — like your parents — lecture every chance they get."

"My father sure does," I agreed. "And lawyers?"

"Stiff, aggressive, rational, and sharp as wasps when they need to be. The worst thing about my first husband was that I lost almost all of our arguments. He was so logical and thorough . . . sometimes I wanted to scream. But I couldn't because when someone is arguing with you in a calm, point-by-point fashion, all you can do is play their game or come off seeming immature."

Driving back to her apartment, I thought over everything Peg had said. "Why do you even want to get married again?"

"Almost all single people do," she said, "even if they say they don't. It's lonely being by yourself. And for a woman my age to find a nice single man with a good career . . . is not that easy." She parked and turned off the lights. We sat in the car for a moment. "But I wish

Arthur did something else. Something creative . . . or at least had a wild streak. Like if he climbed mountains or flew airplanes or wore loud ties that clashed with his shirts now and then. But Arthur is Arthur, and you can't marry someone and expect to change them."

"That's probably true," I agreed.

We got out of the car and headed for her building. "Do you know what your mother always used to tell me, when we were roommates and we used to talk about men?"

It was hard for me to imagine my mother as a single college girl. "What?"

"That I was hopelessly romantic and bound to be disappointed. She used to say that as long as a man is decent and has a good heart, a woman can find a way to make him her perfect love. That it's not the man, but what you make of his good qualities."

We headed up the stairs and into her apartment. "You don't agree?" I asked.

"I wouldn't have married your father and settled for a life as a teacher in the New Jersey suburbs," Peg said. I guess she could tell by the look on my face that she had surprised and even angered me, because she quickly added, "Not that it hasn't been good for your mother. She's a lucky woman. And I love your father dearly, and respect him. But she was a shooting star when she was young. Your mother was the prettiest, classiest, smartest of all of us. There was a zillionaire who wanted to marry her. From one of the richest families in Chicago. She could have had anything. . . ."

I knew I should have been angry at Peg for talking badly about my father, but for some reason I only felt sorry for her. "Good night," I said.

"Thanks for coming out with me."

"I'm sure you'll find the right guy. Whether it's Arthur or someone else."

"More likely I'll end up all alone, like your mother predicted," she said with a laugh. "You go get some sleep."

I went into my room and lay back down in the bed. I thought of my mom, in college, the way Peg had described her. The prettiest, classiest, and smartest. Pursued by zillionaires. And Mom had chosen to spend her life with a high school history teacher.

In my mind I compared small-town, dependable Eric with the star quality of Tommy Fletcher. A French horn player against a superb athlete. A guy who was heading to the Jersey Shore with his family against a guy who spent his summers starring in movies. It seemed like they couldn't possibly have less in common.

As I fell asleep my last thought was that I knew which of them Peg would choose, and that was somehow a little worrying.

CHAPTER 12

On the day that Tommy and I were going to spend together surfing and practicing our scenes, I woke up very early. In fact, it was still dark out. I guess maybe I was a little nervous.

Careful not to make any noise that might wake Peg up, I headed into the kitchen and made myself two toasted English muffins with strawberry jam and a cup of tea. I sat at the glass table in the kitchen, nibbling the muffins, sipping the tea, and running through all my scenes one last time. It's hard to get any kind of real feeling for dramatic material when you're reading all the parts yourself. But at least I had all my lines down. Now and then I dropped a word or twisted a phrase, but in most of the scenes I was letter-perfect.

When I had finished my last scene, I went to the living room balcony and studied the morning critically. One nice thing about Los Angeles is that you don't have to worry about rain or fog. Almost every morning since I had arrived had been sunny and lovely, and this one was no exception. A good day for a get-acquainted drive with my costar.

I was surprised at how often I caught myself glancing at the clock. Would he call or just come by in that spontaneous way of his? Relax, I told myself. This is just a day of becoming friends and rehearsing scenes. But I'm not a good enough actress to completely fool myself, and as the sun got higher my tension level rose with it.

I took a long and relaxing shower, and then debated what to wear. Denim shorts and a V-necked T-shirt seemed like a good, casual choice for a day at the beach. Deciding on a bathing suit was a little more problematic. I had brought a yellow bikini with me, but Eric's face looked out at me from the small photograph on the bedside table, and in the end I put the bikini back in its drawer and packed my more conservative blue Hawaiian one-piece. I also packed some slacks and a favorite blouse, in case I didn't get to come home and change between surfing and heading over to Jason's house.

Tommy came by without calling first, which might have seemed rude for anyone else, but somehow it was almost what I expected from him. He rang the doorbell, knocked, and shouted, "Where are you, girl?" in a loud enough voice for all Peg's neighbors to hear. Peg was eating her breakfast. I was sitting on the couch, reading the morning paper. I stood up and we glanced at each other. "Why don't you let me get it?" she said. "Sit back down and relax."

I sat back down but I don't know if I relaxed.

More ringing and knocking and shouting sounded from the outside hallway. "I hope he's not drunk," Peg said, and walked to the door. She opened it and began to say, "What's all this noise so early in the morning. . . ." Then she shut up for a second. "Oh, they're beautiful. Liz, come take a look."

I stood up. Peg led Tommy into the living room. He was wearing a black bathing suit, a plain white T-shirt, and worn sandals. In his right hand was a gorgeous bouquet of wildflowers, exploding with bright colors. No man had ever brought me flowers before. "Morning, Lizzy," Tommy said.

I took the flowers from him, smelled them, and sneaked another quick look at him over the top of the bouquet. His bathing suit and T-shirt showed off his broad chest and muscular legs. Behind him, Peg raised her eyebrows at me, as if to say, "This guy is too much."

"Thanks, Tommy. You didn't have to bring anything."

"You're right, I didn't. But what the hell," he said with the killer grin. "Ready to hit the road?"

For some reason I was expecting his motorcycle, but

when we left Peg's building he pointed out an old blue van. "Borrowed it from a surfing buddy," he said. "It steers like a sixteen-wheeler, gets about ten miles per gallon, and has a hundred or so of the worst music tapes anybody's ever heard. What more could we ask?"

"Good waves?" I ventured.

"I got that covered. I'm gonna take you to the best little private surfing beach north of Mexico."

"We're not going around here?"

"I get recognized and people want autographs. But thirty miles north are some great little spots we can have almost to ourselves."

Soon we were on a highway that ran northward, right along the coast. "Pacific Coast Highway," Tommy told me. "You can take it clear up to San Fran." He drove quickly and easily. "Now, that's a gem of a city. Ever seen it?"

"Not yet."

"If we didn't have rehearsal tonight I might kidnap you and take you up there." He smiled at me. I didn't know what to do so I just looked out at the ocean. "But unfortunately our director wants to put us through our paces later on. How was your week?"

I told him about Peg's dilemma with Arthur. "She's right," he said. "Who would want to be married to a lawyer named Arthur?"

"You don't even know him!"

"I don't want to. Lawyers make me nervous. That's

Malibu, by the way. Where lots of famous actors and directors live."

There were fast-food restaurants and a few hotels and shops on either side of the road, but besides that all I saw were what looked like normal two-story beach houses. "Where do all those famous actors and directors hang out?"

"When you have a world-famous face, the last thing you want is tourists driving by your windows with binoculars," Tommy told me. "The richest and most famous live in a place called The Colony, with super security and their own private beaches."

"But if they really want privacy, why do they live in a place as famous as Malibu?"

"Don't approach Hollywood too sensibly or you'll never understand anything," he advised. "They want to be seen and they want to be part of the scene, but they don't want to be pestered. Now, what should we listen to?"

He chose some funky old song with moronic lyrics. "C'mon, sing it, girl."

"I can't." Which is true. I can't keep a tune.

"I said, SING IT!"

"ONLY IF YOU SING IT."

So he did. As if acting talent, perfect looks, and athletic ability weren't enough, God had also given Tommy a terrific singing voice.

After a while I joined in. And we sang it together as the blue van left Malibu.

We cruised northward, following the coastline past Zuma and Point Mugu. Houses and small towns became less frequent, till soon the rocky coastline was broken only by small arcs of sandy beach. Without warning, Tommy slowed slightly as he swung into a turnout, pulled a screeching U-turn, and drove down a hidden dirt road between a tangle of bushes that screened the coastline from the Pacific Coast Highway. "Here we are," he said. "Latigo Canyon. A place you'd never stop at if you didn't know."

It was, as promised, a small and very beautiful beach. One other car was parked where the gravel road met the sand, and I could see two surfers in black wet suits lying on their boards a hundred or so yards out. "Will we have to wear wet suits like that?"

"Not quite like that," Tommy said. "Those are kind of old-fashioned." He slid the side door open and passed out a four-foot-long, foam-rubber Boogie board for me, and a six-foot-plus surfboard for himself.

"Why don't I get one of those real ones?"

"You'll have enough trouble catching a wave just with the Boogie board. Now, these are what they call spring suits." He handed me some brightly colored neoprene shorts and a matching short-sleeve shirt. "Put it on over your bathing suit." I took off my denim shorts and T-shirt, and caught him looking at me unabashedly as I stood there for a moment in my one-piece. "What?" I asked.

"You have an unbelievable body, Lizzy Bird."

111

"A body is just a body," I responded, hurrying to get into the spring suit.

"No, some bodies are just bodies and some bodies are not just bodies. And yours isn't. All those curves of yours look hot enough to melt that neoprene." He peeled off his T-shirt and stood there in just his black bathing suit, waiting for me to look at him.

I looked everywhere else first, but finally I met his gaze and looked at him. There wasn't an ounce of fat. He didn't just have muscles on his arms and shoulders like most athletic guys, but also rippling muscles down his flat stomach. I blushed and looked away quickly.

"What? You don't like the way I look?"

"Of course . . . I mean . . . you know how good-looking you are."

His smile slowly faded to a look of concern. "Then what's wrong?"

"Nothing. Just that . . . we're flirting and we barely know each other. And you've got a girlfriend, and I've got a boyfriend."

"Teri and I broke up," he said very quietly.

"You did?"

"Two nights ago."

I could hear the waves crashing in the near distance. "I hope it wasn't . . . anything to do with what happened between her and me on the set."

"She could be real sweet, but I got tired of making excuses for her every time she exploded at somebody."

He reached into the van and took out some swim fins. "As for your boyfriend back in New Jersey and my flirting with you now and then, I guess that's just the way I am when I like someone. No offense intended." He turned back to face me. "Take these and let's hit the surf."

He showed me how to attach the leash of the Boogie board to my wrist, and then I waded out next to him into the Pacific Ocean. The water on my arms and legs was colder than I expected. We paddled out to a spot a hundred yards or so from shore, where the waves came in as rising swells.

"Okay," he said. "Lie on the board and watch the waves. When you see one you like, kick like crazy to stay on the face of it. If you catch it right, you won't have to keep kicking because at a certain point it'll sweep you up and carry you along. The waves peel to the right, toward the point, so you want to try to steer that way. And after the wave breaks, don't let the soup wash you too close to shore. There are some shallow rocks in there. Any questions?"

"Let me see you do it."

"Okay. But make sure you don't try to catch the same wave as me or one of those other two guys and drop in unexpectedly. That's where accidents happen."

"What about sharks?"

He smiled and looked around. "Don't see any fins right now. But if one attacks, hit it on the nose." He began paddling toward shore, glancing back at the swells coming in. After a few minutes, I guess he saw a wave he liked. He paddled harder, caught it, and in the blink of an eye was rocketing along on the face of it, carving it up left and then right with a lot of quick little turns.

At first I didn't have much luck. Either the Boogie board would shoot out from under me or the wave would break over me. Ten or fifteen times I came close but couldn't kick fast enough to catch one. There were floating masses of kelp to deal with — every few minutes my wrists and ankles would get tied up and I'd have to move thirty or forty feet to escape. Eventually, I started getting the hang of it. I kicked and kicked and caught a wave that swept me up and carried me along at high speed. The wave beneath the board surged like a live animal, and it was thrilling to skim along on the back of it.

I caught another few waves and kicked at and missed three or four dozen more, till my legs were sore and the cold water started to make me shiver. Tommy paddled over. "Looks like you've swallowed enough seawater for one day."

"Even for two days. But it was worth it."

We drove to a cute little seaside restaurant so close to the water that ocean spray occasionally added a little unexpected salt to my french fries. A big mug of hot chocolate thawed me out to the point where I could thank Tommy. "That was really a fun morning. I hope

I didn't spoil it by . . . you know . . . what I said this morning."

"About my flirting with you? Would you like me to be serious all the time?"

"I can't even imagine that."

"Good. 'Cause I like to flirt with you. Everyone should flirt. Even dogs and cats do it. And babies."

"Babies?"

"Watch one sometime, when it wants something." He sat back and took a sip of his hot chocolate. "But you said one reason you're uncomfortable is because we don't really know each other very well. So what do you want to know?"

I hesitated.

"Go ahead. Ask anything."

"How old are you?"

"Nineteen."

"You seem older than nineteen."

"That's because I'm so mature," Tommy said with his disarming grin. "I play eighteen to twenty-four."

"Do you live at home?"

"Normally the place where a person lives is their home."

"I mean, does your family live in Santa Monica, too?"

"No. I have my own apartment."

I sensed that I should let it go, but I couldn't stop myself from asking: "Where do your parents live?"

Tommy looked at me, steady on. "Lizzy, both my

parents died in a car accident in Euclid, Ohio, a couple of years ago, before I came here and took up acting. Would you like more of the details? Like which bones they broke and how much blood they lost?"

"No." I felt myself shiver. "I'm sorry."

"Me, too. Maybe that's enough for now. Unless you have more questions."

"Really, Tommy, I'm so sorry."

He threw down some money and stood up. "Let's go find a place to rehearse. One of the reasons I started acting is because it's a nice break from real life."

CHAPTER 13

The blue van climbed up into the canyon along a steep incline of twisting two-lane road. Now and then the Pacific flashed brightly beneath us, only to vanish as a sharp curve took us momentarily inland. Tommy and I didn't say much. I was still upset over what had happened at lunch, and it seemed like he was, too. He popped a tape into the player, and vaguely familiar songs from years and decades gone by began to chase one another through the van. This time, neither of us sang along.

Near the mouth of the canyon, Tommy turned off on a dirt road. We bounced and rattled along for a hundred yards or so, till he parked and then led the way on foot to a shady clearing. It was the perfect spot to rehearse in — quiet, breezy, and sheltered from the sun's mid-afternoon rays. I didn't ask him how he knew the spot was there.

"So," he said, when we reached the center of the clearing, "ready for *Beach Getaway*?"

"Ready," I mumbled, without too much enthusiasm.

"Let's just talk our way through our scenes once or twice and try out different line readings. Okay?"

"Sure."

He studied my face. "What's the matter, Lizzy?"

"Just that . . . I'm very sorry I asked you so many personal questions."

He took my hand, led me over to a fallen log, and sat us down side by side. "Haven't you heard the expression, 'the show must go on'?" I nodded and he put his arm around me and gave me a reassuring hug. "I like you. Just don't ask any more questions about my family and we'll be fine together. Okay?"

"I won't," I promised.

"Now let's see if you can act, Lizzy Bird. The first time we meet . . ." He took out his script and flipped through it. "Oh yeah, it's in the school cafeteria. And I say to my buddy Pancho, 'Hey, look, that babe from New York just put catsup on a taco.'"

I looked at him and tried to find my character. "'It's really none of your business what I eat or how I choose to eat it.'"

He shook his head and shoulders as if shivering. It almost made me laugh just watching him. "'Who-oo-oo-oo. Chill out, babe. You're frosty.'"

We ran through all the rest of our scenes twice, sitting there on that log. I knew my part by heart, but I noticed that Tommy kept referring to his script. "I get the words down perfect the night before the shoot," he explained when we finished. "Till then, I just kind of rough them in. You're a pretty good actress, Lizzy."

"Thanks. I really don't know what I'm doing."

"Well, it's working. You're right in character, scene after scene. Just make sure that when I speak, you take the time to listen and let what I say register, before you reply."

"I'm rushing it?"

"Give your character all the time she needs to listen and make decisions." He looked at his watch. "We have time to run through our scenes once or twice more, before we have to head up to Jason's. Do you want to try acting them out?"

"Sure. But I don't know if I'll be good at improvising actions."

"Just watch what choices I make and respond to them in character. Tonight, Jason will show us the blocking he wants us to use in the movie."

We went through the scenes again, this time acting them out. It was a lot more fun this way — the need to watch each other and constantly improvise made the scenes come alive. When the script called for me to slap him on the cheek, I barely patted him. "C'mon, hit me," he ordered. "I'm a conceited, brainless, and rude surfer dude and I just insulted you. Whack me like you mean it."

So I hit him a little harder, and he grinned.

A few pages later in the script came our first kissing scene. Following the stage directions, Tommy put his hand around the small of my back and looked into my eyes. "'For a dingy East Coast babe, you sure are pretty,'" he whispered.

"'We should . . . go find where they put the money . . .'" I gasped. My character was supposed to be nervous in the script, and I was almost trembling in real life. Would he really kiss me?

Eric had always asked permission to kiss me, but Tommy Fletcher — acting or not acting — was not one to hesitate. He whispered his next line, "'We got time, babe,'" and bent his head closer and closer. I felt his warm breath on my cheeks and lips, and saw those two blue eyes descending.

Blue eyes . . . gray eyes. . . . I flashed to Eric . . . to his face. . . . He would be down at the Jersey Shore now. . . . Would I want him kissing another woman? . . . I pulled away from Tommy at the last possible minute.

"What is it?" Tommy asked.

"I guess I just wasn't expecting you to kiss me . . . like that . . . right now."

"It's in the script. Page thirty-seven. 'He slowly bends down and kisses her passionately.'"

I nodded. "I know it's in there."

"Listen, Lizzy, we're professional actors, getting paid a lot of money. Kissing like we mean it is part of our job. Acting is a game. It's make-believe. I've probably kissed hundreds of actresses — ones I liked and ones I couldn't stand."

"I know. You're right. But until we get to know each other a little better, could we just for today . . . skip it?"

"We could, but I don't think it would be a good idea," he said. "Because tonight we have to do this scene for Jason, and he's going to want to see some heat between us. And in three days we have to kiss in front of the whole cast and crew, and our efforts will be preserved forever on thirty-five-millimeter celluloid. So we might as well deal with this now. Is it that you don't feel attracted to me?"

I shook my head.

"Do you not like to be kissed in general?"

"No, I like to be kissed."

"So it's your boyfriend back home?"

I was surprised that Tommy would be able to guess such a thing. "Yes. I think that's part of it."

"Try closing your eyes."

"I doubt that will help."

"Just shut them, and relax."

"Now?"

"Now." Tommy moved closer.

I half closed them. He put his hand on the small of

my back and we began the lines again. But this time, as we spoke the dialogue, he very gently touched my face with his left hand. He stroked my eyes fully shut with his fingers. Brushed a few strands of hair back from my forehead with his knuckles. Ran two fingers down the sides of my cheeks, and then over my lips. I could feel myself breathing hard but somehow I managed to keep saying my lines.

We got to the moment of truth. My body started actually trembling against his right hand. He whispered his line, "'We got time, babe.'" Once again, I felt his breath on my lips, coming closer and closer. I shut my eyes tightly. His lips grazed mine. And then he kissed me and I didn't pull away.

Neither did he. The kiss lasted a lot longer than I thought it would. At first he was very gentle, but toward the end he got a little passionate and I surprised myself by kissing him back the same way. Finally, Tommy lifted his head and I opened my eyes and looked up at him. I could feel myself blushing and his blue eyes were shining. "'Well, I guess we're more than friends now, babe,'" he said, giving his line from the script.

And I answered with my next line, in a whisper. "'I guess we are.'"

The darkness was just starting to fall as we set out for Jason's house. "Should we stop for a quick bite?" I asked.

"Don't worry about dinner," Tommy told me. "Jason always has plenty of food lying around. Wait till you see his place up in Coldwater Canyon."

"Nice?"

"His uncle was a big director for years in the old studio days, and Jason inherited quite a spread."

Tommy explained to me that Coldwater is one of a handful of canyons that cuts right through the Santa Monica Mountains, connecting Los Angeles to the San Fernando Valley on the other side. A narrow road led up from Beverly Hills, past hundreds of mansions with tennis courts, to more unusual architectural specimens built on slopes in the foothills. We climbed higher and higher, till we reached the crest of the mountains that divide Los Angeles from the valley. The views to either side were spectacular.

"This is Mulholland," Tommy said, turning off Coldwater onto a road that ran right along the crest. "Best views in Los Angeles. Jason's uncle knew where to build his mansion, huh?" In a minute he left Mulholland, veered sharply onto a long private driveway, and soon we were pulling up in front of a security gate with a little numerical keyboard. Tommy punched in a combination of numbers from memory, and the gate swung open.

The driveway widened out till it had enough space to accommodate twenty cars. Only three were there. Tommy pulled in near them and nodded toward a black Mercedes. "Looks like our producers decided to come and watch."

That wasn't exactly good news. I remembered Arvy and Harold all too well from the crazy meeting at my house in New Jersey. Having them attend my first professional rehearsal seemed like an unfortunate complication. But since there wasn't much I could do about it, I got out of the van and followed Tommy toward the mansion.

Jason himself opened the front door and greeted us. "Welcome, you're right on time," he said, ushering us in. "Liz, you're a good influence on this rogue."

I had never been in a house like that before. It must have cost millions, even back at the time when it was built. The furniture and rugs and oil paintings were sumptuous. There were marble statues and even a fountain running indoors, spouting water out of a cherub's mouth into a shell-shaped basin. High-ceilinged rooms gave way to hallways that opened majestically into even larger rooms.

And then we came to the main living room. It was nearly sixty feet square, with a chandelier that looked like it belonged in an opera house, an enormous stone fireplace, a grand piano, and a sunken area with couches and chairs arranged to take advantage of the view. Arvy and Harold were sitting in plush armchairs in front of floor-to-ceiling windows. Behind them, through the glass panes, the Milky Way sparkled above while a far more brilliant galaxy of lights from the Los Angeles basin glittered below.

"Elizabeth!" Arvy said, rising to his feet and spreading his hands with one of his exaggerated gestures of warmth. For a moment he stood there, seemingly enjoying the position and the pose, a producer outlined for us against the stars. Then he stepped forward and motioned impatiently for me to come closer. "How wonderful to see you again. Come here, my dear, and let me make sure you're as pretty in Los Angeles as you were in New Jersey." As I approached, Harold, dressed in black pants, a black turtleneck, and what looked like a tuxedo jacket, also stood.

Arvy embraced me, and then just as quickly let me go. "Sorry I haven't been able to see you sooner. But since you're arriving in the company of this handsome swain, I suppose you're in good hands." He smiled and looked around the vast living room, as if for inspiration. "And to think, we meet again here, in the upper heavens of Hollywood. A long way from . . ." He glanced at Harold. "What the devil was the name of that place in the Jersey suburbs? Begonia? Symphonia?"

"Leonia," Harold said.

"Ah, yes, Leonia," Arvy repeated, flashing me a quick little smile. "A little garden spot in the Garden State." And then he added, to Jason, out of the side of his mouth: "You should have seen it. Hades on the

Hudson. But I rescued her and brought her here." Without missing a beat, he turned back to me, "And your parents? Your wonderful father?"

"They're both fine."

"Sincere, staunch, yeoman types. Salt of the earth." He glanced at his watch. "Unfortunately, we can't stay for the whole rehearsal tonight. We have another project going up — I can't really tell you anything about it except that it's going to be big." He lowered his voice slightly, as if someone might be trying to listen in and steal the idea. "It's an underwater woman-in-jeopardy story with a twist." Again, he glanced at his watch. "But we do have . . . how long, Harold?"

"Twenty minutes."

"A quarter of an hour to get a flavor, just a mere taste, of what you're going to bring to *Beach Getaway*, Elizabeth. So please, dive right in."

Chairs were moved, couches rearranged. Jason told me to relax — and then suggested that we start with scene eleven. It was an early scene, very funny and easy to do.

"Yes, that's a great scene," Arvy said, "but come over here for a second, Jason. Since we have such little time I want to suggest something."

The two of them conferred in loud whispers while I just stood there, trying not to be nervous. Tommy looked as relaxed as always. I guess he sensed my tension, because he put his arm around me and whispered, "You're a terrific actress. They're gonna love you."

Jason returned from his whispered conference with a slight frown. "Our producer would like to see the first scene we're going to be shooting with you two. That's scene thirty-five." I didn't even need a glance at a script to know that was the scene where Tommy and I kiss for the first time. Jason gave us some quick instructions about where to stand and when to move and how he wanted the scene played. "Ready?"

I took a big breath. Tommy gave me a last, encouraging smile.

"And . . . action."

I blew my second line, but Tommy covered for me. At first I was very conscious of Arvy, Harold, and Jason standing a few feet away, watching us, but Tommy was such a good actor that he somehow slowly maneuvered me into my character. I concentrated on his face, and finally I started to lose myself in the part. . . .

And stayed lost in it, oblivious to the three observers . . . till we reached the very end of the scene.

"'For a dingy East Coast babe, you sure are pretty,'" I heard Tommy say. His right hand slid underneath the small of my back, holding me up.

I fell out of character and my body suddenly felt stiff as a plank. I just couldn't kiss him on the lips with those strange men staring at us. I managed to get out the first two words of my next line, "'We should . . . ,'" and then I started to pull away. Tommy played right along with it, following me with his lips, waiting for me to finish my line.

"'We should . . . go find . . .'" Once again I drew away, and once again Tommy moved right with me.

"'Where they put the money,'" he whispered so softly that I'm sure nobody else heard him.

"'Where they put the money,'" I got out in a final gasp.

Just as he had done in the clearing, he stroked my eyes shut. I concentrated as hard as I could on being the character of Beth, a smart East Coast girl, frightened by bank robbers and attracted to a surfer dude who had just saved her life. An East Coast girl without a boyfriend. In danger. And now in strong arms.

The kiss must have lasted more than a minute. When Tommy finally took his head away, I was so drained and dizzy I didn't recognize the sounds I was hearing as applause at first. But then, as Tommy helped me upright, I did.

Arvy was clapping quickly and enthusiastically, his face beaming. Harold, behind him, was also applauding, although with much less energy. "Wonderful," Arvy exclaimed. "Electric, more than electric . . . what's the word, Harold?"

"Steamy," Harold suggested.

"That's an adjective for a Turkish bath."

"Stupendous," Harold tried again.

"That's a description for a circus elephant. This was thrilling! Heart-stopping! I can see that you two have enough explosive chemistry to detonate a dozen terrific pictures. In fact, I've seen all I need to see here. Come on, Harold. Time to turn our attention to building the shark tank in project number two. This one is clearly on the right track."

As soon as they were gone, Jason apologized to us. "I didn't know they would be here tonight till about half an hour ago, and I didn't want you to have to start off with that scene, but they insisted. The bottom line in Hollywood is that the moneymen get to see what they want to see. As a director I could have fought them, but I sort of have to pick my battles. Luckily, you both played it beautifully."

The rest of our rehearsal was a piece of cake. Jason was nice and very patient — he explained what he wanted simply and clearly while I took notes in the margin of my screenplay. As Tommy and I rehearsed, Jason paced around us, studying different possible camera moves and angles.

"For someone who's never formally studied acting, you do remarkably well," he told me when we were finished. He led us to the kitchen and began laying out all sorts of food from his refrigerator. Chicken. Salads. Cold cuts. "Help yourselves." As we dug in, he said, "My only suggestion to you, Liz, is to make more specific choices for your actions."

"I'm not sure what you mean."

"Let's say you open a door during a shot. You have to know exactly why you're doing it. Is your intention

'To see who's there,' or 'To let some fresh air in,' or 'To open an escape route'? The more you know in your own mind, the clearer your acting will be. There's an acting teacher, Inge Mannheim, who can explain this much better than I can. She's old Hollywood — well into her seventies, and very much the grande dame. It might not hurt you to take a few sessions with her. I'm sure our producers would pay."

I nodded. "I'd like to. Do you think I'll be okay in the movie?"

"More than okay," Jason assured me. "And you two look great together."

Before we left, Jason showed us around his mansion. There was a real Oscar — an Academy Award his uncle had won for directing a movie I had never seen, back in the forties. I held it in my hands for a moment. For such a small statuette, it was remarkably heavy.

On the back veranda, near the black-bottom pool, were two wicker chairs where Katharine Hepburn and Spencer Tracy used to sit when they came to visit Jason's uncle. I sat in Katharine Hepburn's old chair for several seconds. *The African Queen* and *The Philadelphia Story* are two of my all-time favorites, and I hoped maybe some of her acting ability would wear off on me.

It was pitch-dark by the time Tommy and I drove down the hill. He explained that Jason was relatively young for a director. "Jason's uncle's old friends got him his first directing job a couple of years ago," he said. "The more time you spend in Hollywood, the more you realize that all the wheelers and dealers in show business have some relative or powerful friend to help them break in."

"You don't," I pointed out.

"I'm not a wheeler and dealer in Hollywood, Lizzy Bird," Tommy told me. And then with a smile, he added, "At least not yet."

He drove me to my building, helped me out of the van, and walked me to the front door. "Quite a day," he said. "From surfing to a Hollywood mansion."

"I had fun, Tommy. But I should go up now."

I tried to step away, but he grabbed my right hand and tugged me gently back. He put his arm around me and looked into my eyes. "Why are you in such a hurry?"

"It's just that . . ."

"We smooched so much tonight, it feels kind of natural to add one more, before we say good-bye," he said, pulling me a little closer. "Doesn't it?"

"Yes, but . . . this isn't acting anymore," I said, pulling away from him with my head, even while my arms were rising, as if of their own accord, to circle his back.

"I like you more than I've liked a girl in years," Tommy Fletcher whispered. "You're so fresh and honest. . . ."

I resisted for two or three more seconds, and then closed my eyes and let him kiss me. It was like diving into a lake in total darkness, thrilling and scary, and I wanted to go deeper and at the same time come up for air. When we finally broke apart, I was surprised to find that I was crying.

Tommy saw my tears and let go of me. "What is it?" He sounded very concerned. "You didn't want to? I'm sorry. . . ."

"No, I did want to. I have to go now. Good night." I broke away from him and, swaying with a kind of dizziness, I climbed the stairs to Peg's apartment. She was already asleep. When I looked in the bathroom mirror my eyes were red and puffy. I just couldn't re-lax — I kept pacing around the apartment for the longest time. It's a terribly confusing thing to feel happy and sad at the same time.

Before I got into bed, I took the photograph of Eric down from the bedside table, looked at it a final time, and put it in my suitcase.

CHAPTER 14

An old-fashioned ceiling fan rotated very slowly above a floor of polished pine. One of the walls was plasterboard, but the white material was almost completely hidden by thousands of eight-by-ten photos of actors and actresses who I guess had studied here in years past. The other three walls were mirrored. I stood in the center of the room, watching my own reflection as a regal woman in her seventies touched my chin lightly with her index finger and elevated it.

"My mother was the most beautiful woman in Europe," Inge Mannheim told me, as if it were her usual conversation starter. "When I was sixteen I eclipsed her in beauty. She never got over it. Relax your neck, Elizabeth." She turned my chin this way and that, studying my profile in different lights. "My dear, you can't know," she continued, studying my features intently while she talked. "Princes and counts climbed over each other to give me the keys to their castles."

"Why did you come to Hollywood and become an actress?" I asked.

"Because Hollywood in those days was the most glamorous place on earth, the true royal set. Who wanted to be cooped up in a castle in Schleswig-Holstein when you could be sipping champagne and trading banter with John Huston, Errol Flynn, Howard Hughes, Lauren Bacall, Audrey Hepburn, Bill Faulkner, Bette Davis, night after night."

"Did you really know them?"

She drew herself up. She was still a magnificently glamorous woman, with high cheekbones, perfectly styled white hair, and big, shimmering, ebony eyes. "Darling," she said, "they knew me. Now then, you're quite pretty enough." She picked up a clipboard and a pencil. "Age?"

"Sixteen."

"A good age. See if you can stay at it for two or three years. Weight?"

"A hundred and eleven."

"Pounds? Kilos? Tons?"

"Pounds."

"In matters other than age, always be precise. Height?"

"Five six." She looked at me. "Five feet six inches."

"Have you studied classical music or ballet?"

"Jazz dance. And I can play some guitar by ear."

She frowned and scribbled on the pad, mouthing

the words out loud. "No dance training. No music. Do you speak any foreign languages?"

"I studied French for a year."

"In France?"

"At my high school in New Jersey."

"No foreign languages," she said, scribbling again. "I assume you haven't traveled abroad?"

It wasn't much fun to hear her discount everything in my background, but she was so imposing that I went on answering her questions. "Yes, I have, during summer vacations. To Mexico and once to Europe."

"Do you have an ambition outside acting?"

"I'm going to be a veterinarian."

The corners of her lips lifted in a strange little smile. "And take care of all the lost puppies and kittens with pains in their paws?"

I didn't like it that she was making fun of me, but I was so afraid of her that I only replied in a soft voice, "Maybe some more serious cases, too."

"I take it you're never been married?"

"I'm only sixteen."

"My dear, I received four proposals the day I turned fifteen. And two of them were decent. Never engaged?"

"No."

"Has any fellow jumped your bones yet?"

"I don't understand."

She lowered the clipboard and enunciated very clearly. "Are you a virgin?"

I looked back at her. "Excuse me, I don't think that's any of your business."

I was afraid she might get mad, but she seemed to enjoy my show of spunk. "You have been given a part in a love story," she said, looking me right in the eye. "I have been retained to teach you how to play the part. To tune the violin, one must know the instrument." She walked in a slow circle around me. "But don't bother answering. I see that what we have here is a dew-fresh little kitten from the provinces. Fur silky. Eyes aglow. Too bad you walk like you want to leave footprints in my floor."

"I walk the way everyone else does."

"Everyone else in this declining culture tramps around like so many dinosaurs headed for extinction. This is how you walk."

And then she did a remarkable imitation of me walking across the floor. She swung her hips carelessly, slouched with her shoulders the way I do sometimes, and looked for all the world like a sixteen-year-old. I was amazed, and I had to stop myself from laughing.

"And this is how I walk." She paraded elegantly up and back. "Do you see a difference?"

"Yes."

"Good. Seeing is the first step to learning. And since I need to learn how far we have to bring you in the six lessons your producer is willing to pay for, let's read a few scenes together."

I was intimidated, but it turned out to be much more fun than I had thought. She was really a wonderful actress, and playing a male surfer dude part seemed to delight her. She found all kinds of nuances in Tommy's lines, and soon we were moving around the empty studio, improvising actions. When we finished, she excused herself to get a glass of water, and then came back and had me sit down on a bench next to her.

"Well, the good news," she said, "is that the Divine Stage Manager gave you more raw talent than you had any right to expect. The bad news is that you haven't really added to that talent, or refined it, even a jot. If we had a year together, I could make you into an actress. In a half-dozen lessons, I can do a good deal less.

"I will teach you how to move more cleanly and be better aware of your body. Remember, every tiny action you make will be immortalized by the photographic process and blown up to giant size for everyone to stare at." I had never thought of it in quite that way before. It was a little scary.

"I will teach you to be more aware of light. If you ever see an actress from my generation — trained in the old studio days — receive an Academy Award, watch how she finds the best light to stand in. It's an art, and these days unfortunately a nearly lost art. The so-called best actresses of today droop themselves against walls, in shadows, like hanging vines. Some of them are good — even quite good, but oh, if only they had had proper training."

She shrugged sadly, as if to say, "what a waste," and went on. "I can show you just a bit about posture. But since you're typecast, appearance and enunciation won't be such a big problem on this shoot. For the most part, we will concentrate on what your director specified: your small and large actions within scenes."

"Do you know Jason?" I asked her.

"His uncle was an admirer of mine. A dear man, and a topflight director. His young nephew seems, at least in this case, to have the same fine directorial instincts — he's quite right, you're throwing too much away by not choosing specific objectives and obstacles for every action. Also, you haven't figured out exactly what your character is thinking before each scene begins, and how she's changed by the end. That forces you to stumble into scenes from twilight and stumble out of them into darkness. All of these choices and preparations are essential, and all can be worked on fairly quickly."

I don't know how much they were paying Inge Mannheim, but she didn't waste a moment of the two-hour lesson. We broke down my script in great detail, and then began with some of the smallest actions I had. I opened jars again and again. I put on a scarf two dozen times. Each time I tried to cheat by not making a choice for even the smallest action, she caught me.

"A string of pearls, darling," she said. "Think of your every word and movement before the camera as a string of perfect, dreadfully expensive pearls. You are threading them through your fingers to show them off, in the best possible light. Do you want to waste even one pearl?"

I shook my head.

"Of course not," she agreed. "Pearls are expensive. Especially when they are given to you, in your innocent youth, by divine providence. Each one is a treasure. The cruel hand of time will snatch them away from you soon enough, but for this shining moment they are yours to show off. Lighting a cigarette, combing your hair, or simply tilting back your head a certain way when you see a handsome-looking fellow enter the room, can make your whole career. It can immortalize you. When do you start shooting?"

"In two days."

"And your costar?"

"Tommy Fletcher."

"Perfect," she said. "He's really quite good."

I didn't know that she knew him. "Was he one of your students?"

"Oh, no. We worked together."

"In a movie?"

"A silly television movie. Unfortunately we were not romantically linked" — she gave me a smile — "so there's no need for you to be jealous. As a matter of fact, I played his grandmother."

"That must have been fun. I would like to see you two act together."

"Many people did. We got quite high ratings. Tommy has an admirable interest in the acting craft. He asked me countless questions, both about technique and also about the old studio days." She paused — whenever she mentioned the old studio days she seemed to lose her breath for just a second. "Yes, yes," she said, recovering, "he'll do quite fine opposite you. I quite approve. My, Elizabeth, but you are a lucky girl."

Aunt Peg surprised me by showing up at the end of my acting lesson with a man in tow. He was tall and a little clumsy, with big hands and a self-effacing smile. His conservative jacket and tie left little doubt in my mind as to who he was. "This is the lawyer who wants to make me miserable for thirty years," Peg told me by way of introduction as we headed out of the acting studio.

"I think forty years of happiness is more what I have in mind," Arthur said. "It's nice to meet you, Liz. I don't get a chance to meet too many movie stars."

There was something solid and old-fashioned about Arthur. He had a gorgeous car — a big Lexus sedan with leather seats. I settled into the backseat and let the air-conditioning wash over me.

"We watched the very end of your lesson through the doorway," Peg told me as we headed away into traffic. "That's quite an old battle-ax."

"I sort of liked the old girl," Arthur said.

"Me, too," I agreed. "She's lived a full life. And she

sure knows everything about acting." I looked out the window. "This doesn't look like the way home."

"It's not," Peg agreed.

"Where are we going?"

"To a boring party."

"One of the partners at my firm is throwing a bash," Arthur told me. "There should be great food. Peg says you've been moody lately, so we thought we'd kidnap you."

"Besides the food, there'll be lots of fascinating conversations to listen to," Peg said with thinly veiled sarcasm.

Arthur glanced at me in the rearview mirror. "Your aunt doesn't like my profession," he said with a nervous little laugh.

"I just don't like being bored."

"But you're willing to come to the parties and eat the free food."

"As long as it's good, why not?"

I stayed out of it and just enjoyed the cool ride as the luxury sedan cruised through Beverly Hills into Brentwood and finally pulled up in front of a Spanish-style house. A maid in a frilly uniform greeted us at the door and led us through the elegant interior to the large backyard. An impressive buffet had been set out on tables near a swimming pool. Forty or fifty men in suits and women in dresses helped themselves to Swedish meatballs, stuffed chicken breasts, seafood pasta, and a variety of salads.

"I'm not really dressed for this party," I said.

"I warned you . . ." Arthur began to say to Peg.

"Nonsense," Peg shot back. "This is Los Angeles. She's dressed fine. Just dig in."

There didn't seem to be anything else to do, since we were already there, so I followed her to the buffet table and dug in. We took our plates over to a picnic table, and were soon joined by two of Arthur's coworkers. For the first time I sort of began to understand a little bit of what bothered Peg about the prospect of marrying into this scene. The two men who sat down with us seemed nice enough, but they soon started talking about a case that they were all working on, and it was like they were speaking in a foreign language. Peg and I couldn't really contribute, since we didn't speak the legal language, so we just ate in silence and then went off to find desserts.

"What do you think of Arthur?" she asked.

"He's really nice, and I can tell that he loves you."

"And what did you think of our table conversation?"

I rolled my eyes, and she smiled. "You have no idea how much of that I've put up with in my life."

After the meal, I sort of wandered off around the grounds and found a secluded bench to sit on that gave me a good view of the party going on in the main part of the backyard. I watched Arthur and Peg mingling and saw how proud he looked to have her on his arm. Peg was obviously making an effort to be a good date for him — she was joking and smiling and making small talk with whomever Arthur steered her toward.

It was nice to be alone for a few moments in a hidden spot in that lush yard. My summer in Los Angeles seemed to be going by so fast that I rarely got a chance to sit back and take a breath. In two days I would start shooting my scenes in *Beach Getaway* — I had a feeling that would be like getting on a roller coaster.

Tommy and I would be together mornings, afternoons, and evenings. On one level that sounded very exciting. Just thinking about him made my heart thump a little faster. But also, spending that much time with him sounded a little scary. He seemed so adult, confident, and independent for a guy who was still a teenager. And I knew so little about him, beside the fact that he was a superb athlete and that he had lived through a personal tragedy.

I told myself that maybe what had happened to his family had made him so mature and self-sufficient. I tried to imagine how I would react if my father and mother were suddenly killed in an accident. It was too horrible to even think about. Even after a few years, I would never, never, be able to recover the way that Tommy had. Thinking about his independence made me admire him and feel sorry for him at the same time.

Eric and his family would be heading down to the Jersey Shore this weekend. Eric didn't even have his driver's license yet — his father would do the driving down to the shore while he sat in the backseat with his obnoxious little sister. Tommy handled motorcycles and vans with ease. It was confusing to have feelings for two guys, less than two years apart in age, whose lives were so different. The more I thought about them, Tommy seemed like a mysterious and in some ways frightening man, and Eric like an endearing and harmless boy. I felt trapped in between.

"So all that legalese drove you into hiding?" Arthur asked.

"I looked up. He was standing there, a drink in one big hand while the other hand was buried a little awkwardly in his pocket. "Mind if I sit down for a sec?"

"No." I slid over and he sat down next to me.

"Your aunt is being given a tour of the house, so I thought I'd wander out here and track you down." He finished his drink in one long gulp. "Sort of gives me a chance to recruit an ear in the enemy camp."

"You seemed like you were doing okay without my help."

He shrugged. "You know I want to marry Peg. Very much."

I nodded.

"I'm forty-three and I've never been married. Close a few times, but as they say, close only counts in horseshoes and hand grenades. I'd like to do it the old-fashioned way. No prenuptial agreements. No separate bank accounts. An engagement. A big wedding. Share and share alike. Kids and a house later on. Maybe even a sheepdog. The whole deal." He stopped talking and looked at me.

"I'm not sure what you're asking me."

"She hasn't said yes."

I looked down at the carpet of ankle-length grass that led away toward the buffet table. It shimmered with water droplets in the afternoon sunshine — a gardener must have hosed the whole lawn just before the party.

"But she also hasn't said no."

I didn't know what to say so I just kept looking down, at the tips of my shoes.

"She says she's thinking about it. What's to think about? You either want to marry someone or you don't."

I finally raised my eyes and looked at him. "I agree with you."

"Of course you do. You seem very sensible. And I know how much Peg admires your mother. So I wanted to tell you . . . assure you . . . that my love is sincere."

"I don't think anyone doubts that."

"And I thought that maybe, once we got to know each other, you and your mom might be able to talk some sense into that crazy woman. Tell her she shouldn't make me wait like this. It's destroying my work habits. Keeping me up at night. Friends ask me what's going on and I don't know what to tell them. I've lost seven pounds." He caught himself. "I'm sorry . . . I didn't mean to unload on you like that."

"It's okay," I said. "But I can't convince Peg to do anything. She makes all her own decisions."

Arthur slowly nodded and rubbed his eyebrows with his palms. "I know," he said. "She seems flighty, but she's actually very strong. That's one of the things I love about her. How old are you, Elizabeth?"

"Sixteen."

"When I was sixteen, the only problem I had was trying to catch line drives in left field." He smiled wistfully, shook his head, and stood up. "Enjoy it while you can. Life turns into a tangle pretty quickly." His big hands hung down awkwardly. He tried stuffing them into different pockets, and then pressed his palms together in front of his body as if he were trying to squeeze something between them. "It was good talking with you. I'd better go find your crazy aunt before she sets something on fire or pushes a lawyer into the swimming pool."

I watched him walk off, stepping carefully on slate stones rather then swishing through the ankle-length grass, and somehow I had serious doubts that Peg would ever agree to marry him. It made me sad to think that, because I liked Arthur.

CHAPTER 15

"Relax," Anna, the makeup woman, said.

"Do I seem tense?"

"Ready to shatter. It's only a movie."

Somehow that wasn't much comfort. Anna was a big-boned Italian woman in her early forties, with shocking-orange lipstick and incredible long black hair that seemed to fall almost to her leather boots. She had her own trailer, filled with containers, tubes, and vials of just about every type of cosmetic substance imaginable. "Give me your arm," she said.

I was in my basic costume, denim shorts and a light top. I held out my arm and she took my wrist and flipped my arm over. "First we need to find the right base for you," she said.

"Why do you use that part of my arm?"

"It's the least tanned, so it's closest to your natural skin color. You have very bluish skin."

"I do?"

"No one's ever told you that before?"

"No."

"It's obvious. Let's try this." She dipped her fingers into a vial containing a flesh-colored base cream. "And this one. And . . . we'll mix in a bit of this, too." When she had the mixture she wanted, she rubbed it on my inner arm, and then studied it, comparing it to my hands and face.

"What do you look for?" I asked.

"We want the color of your cheeks and forehead to match the back of your hands," she said. "Now, let's try a little of this. . . ."

When the base was all on, she put on some powder. "Translucent powder that matches the base," she told me. "Once I have the base, picking the powder's no problem. And some powder blush . . ."

I watched her work and tried to relax. Outside the trailer, I knew that nearly a hundred people were getting ready for my first shot in the movie. In twenty minutes or so, I would have to emerge from this trailer and kiss Tommy on the lips, again and again, in front of dozens of complete strangers and a 35 mm camera. Anna was right — I was petrified.

Earlier this morning, for more than half an hour, we had done a run-through of the shot, setting the marks and locking down the blocking. The number of people and the equipment all around was intimidating. Even though Tommy and I hadn't done any real acting,

I had trembled through nearly the whole experience. Then Jason sent the "First Team" — that's what the stars are called — in for makeup and hair. As Anna worked on me, the technical people were making all the camera and lighting adjustments with stand-ins. There was a girl named Polly, just about my size and weight, who was out there hitting all my marks, again and again.

Anna finished with an eyebrow pencil and began using eye shadow on my lids. "You have nice skin," she said. "Never had a problem with acne?"

"Not really. I guess I've been lucky that way."

"Relax," she said again. "Honey, you're trembling."

"I've just never done this before."

"Well, I've been around a million movies sets. It might seem frightening or . . . glamorous . . . but it's just a business like any other. The producers wouldn't have spent the money to bring you here if you couldn't do the part."

"You don't think they ever make mistakes?"

She looked at me. "I wouldn't ask questions like that around the set if I were you. Be confident. You're a star."

"I don't feel like a star."

"Well, I'm going to make you look like one. Eyeliner, for the eyes. A little mascara — see what that does for your lashes? And now some lip liner and lipstick. *Violà!*"

"It looks good," I said, almost unable to really study

myself. The contours of my eyes and lips were certainly more pronounced.

Someone knocked on the trailer door. "Yeah?" Anna called.

"We need Liz on the set."

"She's on her way," Anna yelled back. She looked at me sympathetically. "You'd better get going."

"Just let me sit here one second longer."

"Want a gumdrop? They help me relax when I'm tense."

"Okay." She plopped a lemon gumdrop in my palm and I put it in my mouth. I sucked on it, counted slowly to ten, and then stood. "Wish me luck."

"Into the mouth of the wolf," she said. "That's what we say to actors in Italy before they go on."

"Okay, then, into the mouth of the wolf. Let's hope he doesn't chew me up and spit me out."

"I'm coming with you," Anna said. "In case you need powder or a touch-up between takes." We walked out into the bright sunshine and headed for the crowd of people standing near the camera.

Scene thirty-five took place in a lifeguard tower. We had taken over a section of beach, and our crew had removed the front section of one of the towers. The camera had been mounted on a crane so that the cameraman could have his assistants raise and lower him to any angle he needed. Sandbags, camera cases, reflectors, and props were scattered all over the beach. A number of crew members turned to look at me as we got close.

"Scene thirty-five, LET'S GO!" Jane, the chunky assistant director, bellowed. In her overalls, with a fishing hat pulled over her ears, Jane managed to look comical and ferocious at the same time.

Jason intercepted me as I passed the camera position. "How ya doing, kiddo?"

"Okay."

Something about my answer made him shoot me a second look. "Don't tense up on me. Do it just like we did at my house. Remember?"

"Sure," I said. He gave me a little push and I climbed up the ladder into the lifeguard tower and found my first position.

A few seconds later, Tommy climbed up after me. "Hey, Lizzy Bird," he said. "I think we're gonna be in a movie together."

I nodded.

"What's the problem? I can't kiss a girl who looks so scared. Give me a smile."

I tried to smile at him, but it felt like my lips might rip and my teeth might crack. My knees were actually knocking together with fright. He left his position, came over, and put his arms lightly around me. "Look at me." It was comforting to look into his strong and handsome face. My body was trembling. "This is nothing," he said. "That camera's not there. All those people aren't there. It's just you and me on a crazy day at the beach. Okay?"

"I'm trying."

He studied my face very closely. "Who did that to you? Anna?"

"She just finished my makeup. . . ."

"I'm gonna make a little fuss now," Tommy said. "Stars do this every once in a while. You can use it to take a few deep breaths and relax. I'll buy you a little time. Okay?"

"You don't have to make a fuss. . . ."

"I do," he said. "You're shaking with fear." And then he shouted, "JANE!"

"WHAT?" the assistant director shouted back.

"We have to hold the shot a minute or two."

"Why?"

"Anna has to wipe that gook off Liz's face."

"What are you talking about?" Jane asked.

Anna came storming over, her long black hair tossing wildly in the wind. "That's right, what are you talking about?" she demanded, looking furious. "There's no gook on her face, just the perfect makeup for this scene."

"No, there's too much . . ." Tommy began.

"WHAT DO YOU KNOW ABOUT MAKEUP?" Anna shouted at him. "I've been doing this for twenty years! No one, NO ONE, insults my makeup!"

Jason sauntered over in that relaxed way of his, turning his baseball cap to shield out the sun. I guess one quality a good director needs is to always seem cool.

"Jane, get everything else ready for the shot," he said. "We'll take it in a minute or two." Jane took the hint and left, so it was just the four of us. "What's the problem?" Jason asked.

Anna was still in a rage. "I made up Liz for this scene and he says I put too much makeup on her, which is nonsense, idiocy, because I know what I'm doing and I've put exactly the right amount on her that a girl of her complexion needs for a scene in this light. . . ."

Jason cut her off by nodding and raising his palm. "Anna knows what she's doing," he said to Tommy. "And it looks okay to me."

"It is okay, for a normal girl, in a normal scene."

"BUT THAT'S WHAT SHE IS, A NORMAL GIRL IN A NORMAL SCENE!" Anna shouted. "WHAT DO YOU THINK SHE IS . . . ?"

"Quiet, Anna," Jason said. "Tommy, if you have a point to make, let's hear it. Otherwise, we need to take the shot."

"You can take it the way she is," Tommy said. "There's nothing wrong with her makeup. You'll get a decent shot."

"Then why are you making trouble?"

"Because Liz isn't a normal Hollywood actress. Liz is a sweet little girl from . . . some little town in New Jersey. When I kissed her before, in rehearsals, you saw what happened. . . ."

"What do you mean, 'what happened'?" Jason asked. "Stop talking in riddles."

153

"She blushes," Tommy told him. There was a moment of silence after he said it. "It'll be the best thing in the shot. Maybe one of the best, truest reactions in your movie."

"That's true," Jason admitted. "I did notice her blushing in rehearsal, after the kiss."

"Not just a little blush," Tommy went on. "She turns crimson, just like the character would in the story. You typecast her dead-on, and now you're gonna cover all your good work up with base and powder and makeup that Anna put on her."

Jason thought about it for ten seconds. "Anna," he said, "tone down Liz's makeup. And I mean fast."

Five minutes later we were ready to take the shot. The argument and the five extra minutes had helped me a lot. At least I wasn't shaking anymore. When we took our first positions, Tommy gave my hand a squeeze. "Let's nail it on the first take," he whispered.

So we nailed it. When I heard "Action!" and started the scene, the part of my mind that was worrying about the camera and all the people who were watching, abruptly shut off. It was just Tommy and me, and the lines and blocking that we had practiced. Inge Mannheim helped a little, too — I didn't rush my actions but let my character think and react. When it came time for him to kiss me, I didn't break out of character or pull away too much. I just leaned back into his strong arms and let it happen.

The kiss lasted a long time, but Jason didn't call

"Cut" when it was over. So Tommy raised his head and we spoke our final two lines, and then he looked down at me, and I looked back up at him for ten or fifteen more seconds. My lips and cheeks felt warm, and I knew that I must be blushing up a storm.

"CUT!" Jason finally shouted. "That was really terrific. Al?"

The cameraman gave Jason a thumbs-up. "Bang on."

Tommy still held me loosely. "Lizzy Bird," he said in a low voice, "you have some kind of talent."

"Thanks for giving me the time I needed," I whispered back. "I think I would have fainted. . . ."

"You were damn good, when it counted," he said. "If I were you I wouldn't be worried about acting anymore. You're a natural."

Something in his voice made me ask, "Then what should I be worried about?"

He gave my arm a little squeeze. "I don't think you're going to be able to go back to New Jersey at the end of this summer," he whispered. "You're too good. Someone's gonna find a way to keep you in Hollywood."

Before I could even think of a reply to that, Jane called out, "FIRST POSITIONS. LET'S GO. READY FOR TAKE TWO! WE'RE RUNNING BEHIND SCHEDULE!"

CHAPTER 16

It was a big complex of brand-new one- and two-bedroom condominiums, built around a central courtyard. There was a giant S-shaped pool in the center of the courtyard, with deck chairs and lush plants all around it.

"Number seven," Tommy said, stopping at a door and fishing a key out of his pocket. "That's my lucky number." He unlocked the door and held it open for me. I hesitated a second and then walked in, and he followed, pulling the door shut behind us.

It seemed like an enormous space for just one person. Light gray carpeting and white walls gave the apartment a wide-open quality. There were just a few expensive-looking pieces of furniture: an elegant pine dinner table, a black leather couch, and a couple of comfortable-looking chairs that faced an impressive sound system. Sliding glass doors at the rear of the living room led out onto a deck above the courtyard.

"I keep a couple of bottles of champagne cold for spur-of-the-moment celebrations," Tommy said.

"Thanks, but I don't really drink. A glass of wine now and then with the family . . ."

"I don't drink much either," Tommy said. "But we still need to celebrate your first ten days of stardom. Do you know how good you've become?" He walked over to the CD player and popped in a disc. Jazz began to play softly.

"The first day, in that lifeguard tower, I almost fainted. But I guess I've gotten a little more comfortable since then. Ten days have just flown by." I couldn't conceal a proud smile. It's kind of nice when you worry about something, and work at it, and then find out that you can do it a lot better than you ever dreamed.

"That's the smile I've been waiting for," Tommy said. "Kick off your shoes. Come on, Lizzy, let's celebrate a little. Life is too short not to have a good time when you deserve it!"

So I kicked off my shoes and we danced around his apartment, barefoot. First we waltzed. Then, when the music quickened, he spun me and twirled me. "Just follow my lead," he whispered. "That's it. Good. Hey, who's leading who?" The music slowed back down and we ended up cheek to cheek. I didn't know much about dancing, but I could tell that Tommy was really good at it. When the song ended he dipped me far over backwards and then as he lifted me back up, he kissed me.

"It's been fun working with you," he said. "To tell you the truth, that first day I was worried. You looked like you might get sick to your stomach. But talk about getting the hang of something quickly! All of our beach scenes are going to be hot, hot, hot." He kissed me again, and released me. "Come, I'll give the star actress the grand tour. I've been here a little less than six months. Here's the bathroom — guess it could use a good scrubbing."

I stuck my head in and gave it a quick inspection. "It's not so bad."

"I'm not one of these guys who doesn't know how to clean up after himself. It's just that we've been working every day. And here's my bedroom." He swung the door open and saw me hesitate. "It's part of the grand tour."

I knew that he could see my nervousness. Tommy picked up on things like that very, very quickly, and it was best to be honest with him. "I've never been alone . . . in a guy's apartment before."

"You're not alone. I'm with you." Without any warning, he shot an arm around my hips, picked me up off the ground, and carried me into his bedroom. He set me down gently on the rug. "Now I've got you in my bedroom, Lizzy Bird, and I'm not going to attack you, so you can just relax."

I tried to stop being so stiff. "It's not that I don't trust you. . . ."

"If I were you I wouldn't trust me. But since I'm me you don't have anything to worry about," he said with one of his raffish grins. And while I was still trying to figure that out, he asked, "Ever sleep on one of these?" He kicked the corner of the bed, which was really a large mattress on the floor.

"No." I turned my head away from the mattress and a glint of gold caught my eye. "Wow, did you win all of those?"

His bedroom had an enormous closet, and stacked in the back of one side of it were dozens of sports trophies. I glimpsed what looked like football trophies and baseball trophies and maybe even a few basketball trophies all mixed in together.

Tommy seemed embarrassed that I had seen them. "Yeah, I won those . . . but it seems like kid's stuff now. I should just give them away to some garage sale or something."

"No, you shouldn't. They're part of your childhood."

He slid the closet door closed, shutting off my view of the forest of gold and silver trophies. "About a year ago, I sold my bed and bought this in Little Tokyo for a hundred and fifty dollars," he said, drawing my attention back to his mattress. "It's a Japanese futon."

"I've seen them before. I've just never slept on one."

"I always felt unnatural sleeping two feet above the floor. Futons make more sense. They give you more support. They're great for sleeping and for . . . lots of things."

I looked at his grinning face and took a half step toward the door.

"See if you like the way it feels," Tommy said. "Go ahead and lie down on it."

"I can tell from here it looks very comfortable."

He lay down on the top of the coverlet, so that he was looking up at me, and held out a hand. "Come here, Lizzy Bird. I'm not going to bite you."

"Tommy . . ." Jazz filtered in from the living room.

"Think of it this way," he said. "If I had a horse in here, and you'd never ridden on a horse before, I'd tell you to get on it. But I don't have a horse in here — I have a futon. And you say you've never laid down on one before. So, I just want you to feel what it's like. Now, come."

I barely heard what he was saying, and I certainly didn't understand it. I got tangled up in those blue eyes, I took his hand, and the next thing I knew we were lying side by side on the futon. "Comfortable?" he asked.

I shook my head.

"See how firm it is?" he asked, rocking his body up and down. The futon barely moved. I rocked my body up and down two or three times, and then nodded.

"You're looking at me like you think I might bite you," Tommy said.

"I just feel . . . uncomfortable. Can we go now?"

"Absolutely. Whenever you want." He slipped his arm underneath my neck, so that my head was resting on his shoulder. "I want to tell you something," he whispered. "Are you listening?" His free hand had somehow come to rest on my stomach.

"Yes."

"I'm not a sex maniac and I'm not going to attack you or try to make you do anything that you don't want to do. I really respect you. I want to be your friend. And I really don't want you to think of me as some kind of a sleazy Hollywood makeout artist. Do you believe that?"

I nodded, but instead of saying yes, I said, "Maybe."

Tommy laughed. "Okay, how about this — I'm a healthy, hardworking, single young guy and I'm attracted to you 'cause I think you're beautiful and talented and fun to be with."

"And I'm attracted to you," I told him honestly. "You're handsome and very talented, too. I'm just not ready to be in a situation like this with you. So can we. . . ."

"You and your boyfriend back in New Jersey never even fooled around, did you?"

"I don't want to talk about him."

"I don't want to talk about him, either," Tommy

said. "Sure, we can go anytime you want. The thing is, tonight is a night to celebrate. And do you know how I'd like to celebrate?"

"I think I can guess."

"You have a dirty mind, Lizzy Bird."

"Tommy, we're alone in your apartment. In your bedroom. On your bed."

"It's more comfortable than the couch," he said.

"And you have your arm around me."

"We're friends. I like to be close to my friends."

"And I have the strangest feeling that any second you're going to try to kiss me."

"Well, some people might say you wouldn't be lying next to me on my bed if you didn't want me to," Tommy said with a smile. And suddenly, I don't know quite how, he was kissing me and I was kissing him back. At first he was very sweet, but soon he began caressing me through my blouse. When he began to undo the buttons, I said, "Tommy, please don't. . . ." A few minutes later when his hand slipped inside my shirt I said, "Stop." And then, again. "Stop!"

He took a deep breath, and rolled away from me. "Okay," he said. "Sorry. I really like you."

"I like you, too."

We lay there, maybe a foot apart, listening to the jazz that was still playing. Gradually, our breathing got a little bit more normal.

"Lizzy, you tell me, what would you like to do?"

Tommy asked. "What's your idea of celebrating?"

I thought about it. "We've been working together for ten days and I don't feel like I understand you at all," I said. "I know I can't ask you personal questions, but show me what makes you tick. What do you like to do when you have free time?"

"Act."

"In your free time," I repeated.

"Besides surfing and pickup basketball, I read scripts. Practice scenes for auditions. And some nights I like to try stuff out."

"Try stuff out how?"

Tommy didn't answer. He was normally so open about everything that I found his suddenly pulling back at my question kind of intriguing. "You're studying with Inge Mannheim, right?" he finally asked.

"I've just had a few lessons."

"She can teach you anything you need to know about the technical side of the craft."

"She says you're a fine actor, too."

"The old mutual admiration society. But there are things she can't teach you."

"Like what?"

"Trying things out and taking real chances."

"I don't know what that means."

He looked at me, and seemed to make some kind of decision. "Lizzy, it's your choice. If you want, we'll get dressed up and go out for a great meal, and do all the normal, conservative, fun things two people do when they celebrate. But if want me to show you what you're asking about, then you'll have to follow my instructions and trust me. It'll be a little frightening, but a much more interesting evening."

"As long as nobody gets hurt," I said. "Show me."

CHAPTER 17

At first I thought that we were going to some sort of masquerade party. Tommy hauled a big carton of men's clothes — some of them pretty wrinkled and rancid-looking — out of his closet and began trying them on me. A red-checkered shirt that looked like it belonged on a deer hunter struck him as just the thing. "It's way too small for me, so it'll be just a little too big for you," he said. "Roll up the sleeves and it'll be perfect."

"Perfect for what?" I asked, obediently rolling up the sleeves. "Are we going after moose or elk?"

"Your blue jeans are too new and too sexy, but they'll have to do. The biggest problem is your face and hair. I can't mess up your hair or Jason will kill me. Let me think on it for a minute, while I get dressed my-self."

Tommy got into faded green work pants with a dozen or so pockets, and an old blue sweater that smelled faintly of fish. "Where did you get these clothes?" I asked, sniffing pointedly.

"The Salvation Army," he said. "This sweater must have belonged to someone who worked on a fishing boat. I washed it twice, but the smell's into the fabric like a stain — it won't wash out."

"Tommy, where are we going in these outfits?"

He looked at me and snapped his fingers. "I got it — we'll just cover your hair up with one of my biker kerchiefs." He took red and blue kerchiefs out of the top drawer of his dresser, and tied the red one around my forehead and behind my ears in such a way that it hid most of my hair. With the oversized hunting jacket hanging outside my jeans, I looked grungy with a capital "G."

Tommy tied the blue kerchief over his own long straw-colored hair, and then took a pair of eyeglasses with heavy black frames out of a case. "No matter what clothes I wear, people recognize my face," he explained. "But as soon as I put these on" — and he did — "no one knows me."

He was right. With the blue kerchief covering his hair, the old-fashioned glasses balanced on the bridge of his nose, and the stinky sweater on his back, I probably wouldn't have recognized him if I passed him on the street.

"Let's see the happy couple," he said, leading me over to a full-length mirror. We stood side by side. "What do you think?"

"We look and smell like we live on the streets."

"Bingo," he said. "We just need a few props." He piled the remaining old clothes from the carton into a canvas bag, zipped it up partially, and handed it to me. "For myself, just the Good Book," he said, taking a well-thumbed Bible down from a shelf. "Okay, I think we're ready, Lizzy Bird. Let's hit the road."

"What road?"

Instead of answering, he just ushered me quickly out.

We took his bike and headed west, toward the beach. When we got to Ocean Avenue he turned south, following the shoreline a mile or so to the border between Santa Monica and Venice. Venice is a slightly poorer and more dangerous town than Santa Monica. The colorful kooks who hang out on the famous Venice Beach during the day roam around at night, and some of them commit crimes. Tommy stopped on a dark street in the middle of nowhere and locked his bike up carefully. "We'd better walk from here."

"Tommy, I'm getting nervous."

"Me, too," he said. "Isn't it a great feeling to have once in a while?"

"Whatever it is that we're doing, have you done it before?"

"Not exactly."

"Are we going to visit friends of yours?"

"Lizzy, you said you wanted something different, remember? Okay, that's what you're going to get."

The street seemed narrow and cloaked in shadows. I wouldn't have felt safe in such an area alone. Even with Tommy by my side it seemed ominous. Soon we turned onto a street with stores. Two dozen or so homeless people were hanging out in doorways or sitting on the curb. It wasn't just men — there were women and children, too.

A sign a hundred feet up caught my attention. It said, BACKSTREET MISSION. "We're not going in there?" I asked.

Tommy glanced at his watch and then took my hand. "Here's the story, Lizzy Bird," he whispered. "Ready?"

"For what?" I asked.

"We got married young. Came down to the city from up north. A mill closed, I lost my job, and we started traveling around looking for work. We got into LA this morning on a bus and walked over here."

The door to the mission was pushed open. A tall man stepped outside and shouted, "Come and get it." The homeless people who had been lounging around outside all got up and started following us toward the door.

"Tommy, I don't want to. . . ."

"You need a good meal as badly as I do, baby," he said, tugging me in through the door. "To get our strength back."

The crowd of hungry people behind us sort of

forced us in. I ended up holding tightly to Tommy's hand and following him down a long hallway. The walls were painted lime-green, and the floor was yellow-and-black-patterned linoleum, discolored in spots. The crowd pushed us quickly along, till we funneled out of the narrow hallway into a large dining space. Folding chairs had been set up around six or seven round wooden tables.

Two big pots of food sat on a table at the front of the dining room. A stout woman and the tall man who had summoned us in from the street donned aprons and began ladling out food into plastic bowls. The throng of homeless people formed a line, and soon Tommy and I were passing in front of the food table, holding out empty bowls.

"Evening," the tall man said.

"Evening," Tommy said back. I kept silent.

"Haven't seen you here before," the tall man said.

"That's right," Tommy said, accepting what looked like a bowl of turkey stew from the man.

Then it was my turn. "Hi, honey," the man said. "Got a good appetite, tonight?"

"Yes, sir," I whispered. I felt so guilty about our whole charade that I wanted to scream and run out the door. We didn't belong there, with those poor homeless people and their free dinners. But I didn't have the nerve to do anything except lower my eyes and accept a bowl of turkey stew from the man.

The woman gave us vegetables — peas and carrots — and two slices of bread each. "What's your name?" she asked me with a smile as she handed me the bread.

I couldn't answer or even look her in the eye.

"My wife's name is Lisa," Tommy said, putting a hand on my shoulder and guiding me along. "She ain't feeling too well today."

"A good meal will get her back in spirits," the woman said.

We took our food over to an empty table and sat down. "I want to leave right now," I whispered.

"You need food to stay strong, honey," Tommy said, and then nodded to a toothless old man who sat down next to me at our table and began eating his stew at incredible speed. Soon a mother and her eight- or nine-year-old daughter, a big woman who seemed much too heavy for a small folding chair, and a foul-smelling man in a trench coat also joined us.

Tommy took out his Bible. "Let's give thanks before eating," he said to me in a low, serious voice. He flipped the Bible open, found the page he was looking for, and folded his hands on the table. I didn't know what to do, so I followed his example. To my surprise, the woman and the mother and daughter stopped eating and also folded their hands. The toothless man kept slurping down turkey stew, occasionally glancing at us, and the vagrant in the trench coat appeared to be off in his own hungry world.

"'Out of the depths have I cried unto thee, O

Lord,'" Tommy read. "'Hear my voice; let thine ears be attentive to the voice of my supplications.'"

"Help me, Jesus," the woman whispered. Her eyes were shut tight.

"'If thou, Lord, shouldest mark iniquities, who shall stand?'" Tommy continued. "'But there is forgiveness with thee, that thou mayest be feared.'" He closed the Bible. "Thank you for this food and for the gift of life. Amen."

A few other "Amens" came from around the table, and then we all started eating. The turkey stew was so thin it was more like soup. There were only three or four small shreds of turkey in my whole bowl. But food is food, and the people at our table appeared to be very hungry.

Even though I was very uncomfortable at being there under false pretenses, it was undeniably fascinating to get a firsthand glimpse at such a world. Our table was a study in contrasts. The toothless man finished his stew, picked up the bowl, and drank the last few drops with a sound like a suction machine. He stood up, wiped his mouth with the back of his hand, and left without a word.

The young girl and her mother occasionally spoke to each other in whispers as they ate. I couldn't tell what they were saying — I think they were speaking in Spanish. She looked to be a terribly shy little girl, and I wondered if something bad had happened that had frightened her.

The foul-smelling man in the trench coat kept getting noodles and pieces of turkey and carrot caught in his long beard. He had wild eyes and ate bent over his bowl, with both his elbows on the table.

The big woman seemed to be the most friendly person at our table. After a few minutes she turned to me and asked, "You two're not from around here, are you?"

"No, ma'am," I answered.

"We're from up north," Tommy said. "Came down here looking for work. What about yourself?"

"Born and raised right here in Venice."

"So you got folks nearby?"

"Don't got nobody," the woman said. "'Cept the Good Lord."

The vagrant in the trench coat raised his wild eyes and looked at her. "You got nobody."

She gave him a nasty look. "Why don't you clean yourself up? There's free showers down by the beach."

"Suck off," he shot back.

She wasn't at all intimidated. "Watch your mouth. We have a young one at the table."

"I said, suck off, bitch," he repeated more loudly. He pushed his bowl of stew away and stood. "You and your praying make me sick. He's up there listening to you, huh?" He laughed deep in his throat and rubbed his beard so that a few particles of food fell out onto the table top. "How can people be so damn stupid?" And then he left.

The woman shook her head and then smiled at the young girl. "He didn't mean no harm, honey."

The girl seemed frightened that someone was speaking directly to her. She buried her head in her mother's lap, and her mother stroked her hair.

Our table was quiet after that. I managed to finish most of the turkey stew and was nibbling on a piece of bread when a commotion broke out three tables down. We all turned to look. A younger man was accusing an older one of stealing something. "Give it back or I'll take it back."

"You . . . keep away from me," the older man bellowed. He took a shove in the chest, and then gave one back. Punches were thrown and a chair was tipped over.

The tall man who ran the mission tried to separate them, but he was clearly having his hands full. Tommy got up, walked quickly over to the melee, and put the younger of the two combatants in some kind of hold.

"Git off me, git the hell off me," the young guy shouted, thrashing around, but Tommy was much stronger than him and marched him out to the hallway. The man who ran the mission followed with the older of the two combatants in tow. Shouting and the sounds of pushing and shoving got fainter as the four men moved away down the hallway, till the only sound in the big dining room was the scraping of plastic silverware against plates and bowls.

"You tell your hubby to watch out," the woman

advised me. "That guy he pulled out of here carries a blade."

I had never even seen a fistfight before, and the news that Tommy was wrestling with a man carrying a potentially lethal weapon alarmed me. But a few seconds later Tommy and the manager of the mission walked back in, safe and sound. Their clothes and hair were a little messed up, but beyond that they looked fine and remarkably relaxed. Tommy sat back down at our table, gave me a wink, and without a word began finishing his turkey stew.

The Spanish-speaking woman and her daughter left the table, so there were only three of us left.

"Tommy," I whispered, and nodded at the woman. "She says the guy you were fighting with carries a knife."

"I had a good hold of him," Tommy told me. "He wasn't going to reach for anything."

"You be careful walking out," the woman said. "I know him a long time. He might stay out there waiting for you two to come out."

"Thanks," Tommy told her. "I can take care of my own."

The tall man who ran the mission sauntered over to our table and sat down next to me. He must have been six feet five, and he had a two- or three-day growth of black stubble around his chin. "Hi," he said. And then to Tommy, "'Preciate you helping me."

"It wasn't nothing."

"I saw you reading a prayer before the meal."

"That's right," Tommy said.

"I might know some people who could help you two get back on your feet."

"We'll get back on our own feet and walk out as soon as we finish eating," Tommy told him.

"I was just tryin' to help."

"We don't even like taking free food."

"Not many people do," the tall man said and turned his attention to me. "Where are you from?"

"Up north," I answered, repeating what Tommy had said earlier.

"Me, too," he said. "Whereabouts up north?"

I glanced at Tommy. "Way up north," Tommy told him. "Humboldt County."

"Whatta ya know, that's where I'm from," the tall man said excitedly. "I'm from Red Bluff, near Redding. What about you?"

"We're from a little town nobody ever heard of."

"I know that area backwards and forwards," the tall man said. "Try me."

Tommy was quiet for a second. I looked down at my now empty plastic bowl. He saw me glance down, and put his hand on my arm, as if to comfort me. "We don't like to talk about it, if it's all the same to you," he told the tall man. "Mill went bankrupt, we lost everything, you probably know the story."

"It's a shame," the tall man said. "Didn't mean to pry."

"That's okay."

"Those little towns are dying one by one."

"Like you said, it's a damn shame," Tommy agreed.

"Whole lifestyle is dying with them."

"Only thing to do is move out," Tommy said. "The day we lost our house my baby and I had a long talk. Remember, honey?"

"It wasn't that much of a house to lose," I whispered.

"You keep telling yourself that, if it makes it easier," Tommy told me, patting my arm. "It was about the cutest little cottage you ever wanted to see," he told the tall man and the woman. "Fixed it up ourselves. Built a garage. My baby here painted it. Lots of yard space, front and back."

I listened to Tommy go on, fascinated at his ability to spin out a completely untrue story. His eyes were fixed on some point in the far wall of the mission's dining room, as if he were seeing the little cottage in the forest that we had left behind.

"We were thinking our kids would play in that yard," he said. "Plenty of room for 'em. But anyway, we up and lost it. Just didn't make sense to stay and look for work in a place where there wasn't any. So we said good-bye to her folks — mine don't live in those parts — and we tried Portland for a while. Sacramento.

Frisco, but couldn't find nothing. And now LA. Least the weather's easier here."

"That's the truth," the woman said. "Just, you two be careful. 'Specially if you try sleeping out on the beach. Anything can happen on the sand, after dark."

"You take care of yourself," Tommy told her. "We'll be okay. Now we'd better be going." He helped me up. "Thanks for the food," he said to the tall man.

"You don't have to thank me. Come back for more. You sure I can't help you two find somewhere safe to sleep?"

"We'll be okay," Tommy said. "Won't we, baby?"

"I'm not sleeping out on the beach," I said to him.

"You won't have to, baby. Come on, let's go." We walked back out through the narrow tunnel to the front door, and then exited onto the dark street. Tommy was careful, looking both ways before leading me away from the mission. "I don't think the guy had a knife, and I doubt he would hang around this long," Tommy said. "I bet he's out getting in more trouble someplace else."

When he was satisfied that it was safe, Tommy put his arm around me and we walked quickly down the block. "Hey, baby, you were pretty good," he whispered when we turned onto the street where his motorcycle was parked. "But what did you mean, our house wasn't much to lose?"

"Tommy, whatever made you want to take me in there?"

"It was exciting, wasn't it?"

"In a way," I admitted. "But we had no right to be in there."

"It didn't hurt anybody. And where else can you see a fistfight and hear two down-and-outers discussing God . . . and that poor kid at our table. So scared she almost couldn't eat."

We reached his bike, got on, and he drove me home through the darkness. He pulled up right in front of my building and I got off the motorcycle. When I handed him my helmet, he caught my hand. "Hey, you're not mad at me for taking you there?"

"It made me very uncomfortable."

"It's supposed to," he said. "I haven't gone to that mission before, but I've gone to places like it. And also to ritzy parties where I pretend I'm from another country and speak with an accent, and to political events, and once even to a big seminar for medical students."

"I guess I just don't understand why you do such things. What do you get out of it? Wouldn't it be incredibly awkward if you got found out?"

"Sure would," he said. "That's what gives me a charge. It sharpens me as an actor. Exposes me to things I wouldn't see and hear just going to auditions. Did you see that old guy at our table drain his bowl of stew?" Tommy picked up an imaginary bowl and drained it with the same strange suction sound the toothless old man had made. He set the bowl back down into thin air and smiled at me. "The hardest kind of acting to do is offstage, away from a camera, with no script."

"Is that acting at all?" I whispered. "Those were real people we saw tonight."

"I didn't hurt any of them. But if I made you uncomfortable, I'm sorry. You said you wanted to see, so I showed you. Good night, Lizzy."

I went upstairs and let myself into the dark apartment. Soon I was in bed, staring out through the window at the half-moon. It had been such a strange evening. Tommy had been so aggressive in his apartment, especially when he had carried me into his bedroom, that even thinking back on it scared me. But it thrilled me, too. I had gone over there of my own free will, and I knew I could have stopped kissing him whenever I wanted.

As for the second part of the evening, it was even more confusing to try to sort out. Surely what Tommy and I had done was wrong. Taking food meant for homeless people was wrong. Going undercover to observe people's misery felt sneaky and sleazy. Pretending to be something we were not involved a whole series of lies. Yet, at the same time, it had been exciting and very interesting. And, as Tommy had said, no one had gotten hurt.

As I drifted off to sleep, I remembered what Arvy

the producer had said back in my house in Leonia, about reality being the only rare commodity in Hollywood. "Nearly nonexistent," his assistant Harold had agreed. For the first time I thought that maybe I understood what the two of them had been talking about.

CHAPTER 18

"I haven't gotten to an airport this early in years," Peg complained. I was too excited to reply, and anyway I could tell that she was secretly just as eager to greet my mom as I was.

They attached a walkway, the plane's door opened, and soon travelers were streaming through the gate into the terminal. My mom was one of the first ones out. I ran to meet her and we locked up in a tight hug — it seemed like much more than three weeks since I had seen her.

When I finally let her go, Peg gave Mom a big hug also, and they told each other how well they looked. "The only thing you need is sun," Peg said. "We're going to take you right to the beach."

"I put myself in your hands, Peg," Mom said. "And yours, Liz. Let's all let down our hair and go wild for a week!"

Minutes later we were in Peg's convertible, heading

for Venice Beach. Peg had a grand old time making fun of my mom's pantsuit outfit. "You look like you're going for a job interview at a mortuary."

"And you look like you're modeling underwear for an MTV fashion show," my mom shot back.

"Maybe so," Peg admitted, "but which would you rather be doing? Anyway, I knew how you would arrive, so I brought you a beach outfit."

We left the car in beach parking and soon found a public rest room where my mom could change. Peg handed her a little bundle of clothes. "Just squeeze yourself into these, Katy, and you'll be ready for the beach action."

"I'm afraid to even ask what you have here for me," Mom said with a smile, and disappeared into the rest room. She emerged a few minutes later, in tight and very sexy pink shorts and a skimpy top.

Peg gave her the thumbs-up. "That's a lot of leg you're showing there, Kate baby."

"Where did you buy these clothes?" Mom asked her with a laugh. "At a discount store for prostitutes?" And then to me, Mom said, "Liz, I can already see we're not going to tell your father too much about this trip."

"You look good in those, Mom," I assured her. "Just try not to get arrested."

I was also dressed in short shorts and a bikini top. I figured if I was going to hang out with these two wild women, I had better show a little leg myself.

The three of us headed out onto the Venice Beach

walkway. It was crowded with virtually every human type in every costume imaginable. A man in flowing white robes rolled by on roller skates, strumming a guitar. Super gargantuan bodybuilders, their oiled chests swelling with ridges of muscles like mountain chains, tromped by with platinum blondes in bikinis. There were teenagers and old-timers, skateboard daredevils and roller skaters, policemen on horseback and determined tots on tricycles, all parading down the miles of beach, ogling each other and the bizarre acts on display.

I knew Southern California was full of oddballs, but some of the acts on that beach walkway were about as strange as strange gets. There was a man who lay down barebacked on shards of broken glass, put a wooden board across his stomach, and asked members of the audience to walk on top of him. Next, we passed a couple who had trained their two dogs to howl on cue. They sang folk songs, like "This Land Is Your Land," and at certain key points they would leave words hanging and their dogs would fill in the missing words with long howls. There was a man who juggled chain saws. "If I drop one, it could be rippingly embarrassing," he told the crowd. We all moved back a few steps.

Mom seemed to get a kick out of all of it. When Peg went to get us ice-cream cones, Mom asked me, "Is this the way it is all the time out here?"

"Not quite this crazy, but close."

She heard something in the tone of my voice. "Poor Lizzy."

"It's been fun."

"As long as the compass needle still points to north, as we used to say. . . ."

I thought that over as Peg returned with our cones. We turned back and slowly retraced our steps down the long beachfront promenade. Three handsome young bodybuilders passed us and took a good long look. Peg smiled back at them. "Hi, boys."

"Lookin' mighty fine, ladies," one of them said.

It felt strange to be out with my mother on such a walk down the boardwalk. I was seeing a side of her I had never seen before — it was easy to imagine my mom and Peg going to college dances and attracting lots of attention. Even at forty, Mom had an effervescent friendliness — not to mention great legs — that drew the attention of many of the men we passed. I drew my share of attention, too — at first I felt a little self-conscious at all the glances and whistles and stupid pickup lines, but Peg and my mom seemed to be just playing it for laughs and having fun, so after a while I followed their example and we had a blast.

When we got back to Peg's apartment, my mom showered and began to unpack. The living room sofa folded out into a double bed, so all three of us had our own rooms to sleep in.

I helped Mom hang up her good clothes. "Tell me about this Tommy fellow," she said as she passed me a lightweight cotton dress.

"He's very different from any boy back home," I said, slipping the dress on a hanger.

"Different how?"

"Completely sure of himself."

"He must be handsome, to be a movie star."

"Very," I admitted.

"Tremendously," Aunt Peg called from the kitchen. "Irresistibly." I hadn't even known she was listening.

Mom smiled and lowered her voice. "Have you been able to resist him?"

"I think I've done better than most," I told her with an embarrassed smile.

She finished putting her most elegant black evening gown on a hanger. She was so fastidious when she unpacked, it made me impatient to watch her. "I have a letter from Eric to give to you."

"He sent it to you?"

"From the shore."

"Why didn't he just send it to me?"

"I don't know." She handed me a white envelope. "But here it is. It'll take me ten or fifteen more minutes to finish unpacking. Why don't you go read it by yourself?"

I took the hint and headed into my bedroom. My hand was shaking as I opened the envelope. Inside were a photograph and a letter.

I looked at the photo first. Sunset at the Jersey Shore. I had spent that afternoon at Venice Beach, and it was interesting to realize what a different look and feel East Coast beaches have from West Coast beaches. I could tell that this photo had been taken on a cold and windy evening, and that a rainstorm was on its way. Looking at the swollen June sky in the background, it seemed almost possible to smell the fast-approaching rain. No one was swimming or surfing in the crashing waves.

Eric was wearing a blue windbreaker and standing on the deck of a seafood restaurant in the foreground. He held a big lobster in his right hand, slightly elevated, as if offering it to the camera. The expression on his smiling face was simple to read: "This one's for you."

I must have looked at that photograph for over a minute without so much as blinking. Eric's gray eyes were the exact smoky color of the stormy June sky far above him. His mop of unruly hair was not merely uncombed — it was blown in crazy tangles by a gust of wind. His face was not handsome, but it was tanned and he looked very happy.

Finally, I put the photograph down and read the letter. It was handwritten, on two pieces of typing paper.

Dear Liz,

I got your letter a while ago. Sorry I haven't written back sooner, but as you can see from this photograph, I've had my hands full. Seriously, I'm not a very good correspondent, but

I've been thinking about you all the time. Whenever I pass a movie theater, I imagine your name on the marquee in bright lights and your picture out in front.

It sounds from your letter like you're having a wonderful and fascinating time. I guess you've probably forgotten all about things like rain and flashes of lightning at midnight, and thunder that wakes a person up out of a sound sleep. Well, that's all we've been having for a week. Rain, rain, rain. I've beaten Tammy in every board game under the sun, from Scrabble to Monopoly to Parcheesi. Last night Dad took us to a Bingo night at a local church, and I won that, too. Fifteen dollars for one Bingo. And all the time it poured outside.

We never got to finish our talk by the bus stop about going out with other people. I got the sense that you wanted to, if you met someone, but you were embarrassed to say so to me. You're so sweet.

I never thought I'd want to, but I have to be real honest. I've met a girl — I guess I should say a woman, right? — named Annie. Her family has a beach house close to mine, so in all this rain we've ended up spending a lot of time together. We're not exactly going out but we're not exactly just friends, either, and I wanted to write and tell you that.

Anyway, lots of times when I think about you I feel sure that you'll never come back to New Jersey. You're too beautiful and talented. And you weren't so happy here. I've had time to think about it, and I can understand a bit of what it's like to be asked out to a prom by guys you barely even know, who just see you like some kind of prize. I guess maybe you belong in Hollywood with all the other beautiful people. It certainly sounds like more fun than sitting in a beach house in the rain, telling my little sister not to torture me.

Speaking of my little sister, I would have written to you before, in Los Angeles, but she managed to throw out the piece of paper with your address on it. I can promise you that I pulled some of her hair out for doing such a thing. I would have pulled it all out, but my mom stopped me. Anyway, I got the idea of writing to you and sending it to your mom, which is what I'm doing now.

Bye, Liz. I hope the days are sunny and perfect and the nights are bright with the light from movie stars. Whatever you decide to do, I'm sure it will be the right decision. I'm glad I had the chance to get to know you — it will always be special. Maybe someday we'll eat a couple of these three pounders together, and go through another haunted house with you screaming in my ear. If not, I wish you all the best. . . .

Sincerely,
Eric

Not even "Love." Just "Sincerely." I went back and reread the part about Annie and the neighboring beach houses and "not exactly going out" but "not exactly just friends, either." In my mind's eye, I found myself imagining this Annie. Red hair. A sweet face. Always stopping by to say hello and bake stuff with Eric's mom or help Tammy with her silly projects. And then staying when the rains hit, so that she ended up with Eric, sitting on some old sofa on a back porch. Probably he practiced his French horn and she listened and smiled at him and clapped. Or maybe she played an instrument, too — for some reason I pictured her with a silver flute in her hands. Or a harmonica . . .

"Lizzy?" Peg's voice carried in from the living room. "Ready to go to dinner?"

"Coming in a sec," I shouted back. I folded up the letter and put it in the suitcase next to my other photograph of Eric. Then I hurriedly changed out of my beach outfit. When I walked out into the living room, Arthur was there, dressed too formally as always, exchanging a polite greeting with my mom.

"Arthur's taking us to a seafood restaurant in Malibu," Peg said. "Doesn't that sound like just the thing? Wait till you see this place — movie stars, incredible cars, grilled salmon, Pacific lobster, made-to-order sunsets. . . ."

"I don't know . . . I don't quite feel like seafood. . . ." I mumbled.

"Oh, they have other stuff, too," Peg assured me, and glanced at her watch. "But we have to hurry. We have a seven o'clock reservation. Let's go, everybody."

As we headed down to Arthur's car, my mom took my hand. "Is everything okay, sweetheart?" she whispered.

I forced a smiling nod. And I guess I was becoming a pretty good actress, because my mom said "Good, then let's go check out this Malibu hot spot," and we all hurried off to Arthur's car, with me trailing just a few steps behind.

CHAPTER 19

It's always easier shooting indoors than outside, because you can completely control your environment. The rising and sinking sun won't change your lighting setups, and ambient sound noises like car horns and people shouting off camera won't cause wasted takes.

We had finished the beach scenes, and the week of Mom's visit we were shooting in a high school in Santa Monica. School was of course out for the summer, so we had the whole place to ourselves. The scenes were short and fun — they were the ones where Tommy's beach dude character and the girl I was playing meet for the first time, and where our different personalities are established.

As it happened, the high school we were shooting at was within walking distance of Peg's house. The morning after my mother arrived in Los Angeles, the two of us headed over there together, bright and early to make my call time. "I'm impressed already," Mom

said as we hiked past condominiums fronted by swaying palm trees. "You seem completely relaxed for
someone on her way to star in a movie."

"You should've seen me the first day," I told her. "I
almost didn't come out of the makeup trailer."

"Even so. It's been less than a month."

"Well, I guess I know what to expect, now. Plus . . .
I don't mean to sound like I'm bragging, but I can do
this."

"What?" Mom asked.

"Act in front of a camera with all the lights shining,
and the crew people and extras watching. Keep my
concentration and jump right into character. Lock in a
performance so that it's the same take after take, long
shot and close-up. I'm not saying I'm going to win any
Academy Awards or anything, but at least at this level I
feel like I can give them what they want."

"If you do win an Academy Award," Mom said, "I
know just where we can put it. In the center of the
mantel, and we'll move your father's old golf trophy to
the basement."

I grinned — it was so good to have her there, making fun of the whole movie world. I knew that even a
gleaming golden Oscar like the one in Jason's mansion
up on Coldwater wouldn't blind my parents for one
moment, or turn their heads, or puff up their egos.
Sure they would be proud of it, but they probably
would put it up next to a golf trophy and make jokes
about it to their friends.

As we neared the school, I began to walk a little faster. "Are we late?" Mom asked, speeding up to keep the pace.

"No. Right on time." I had been looking forward for weeks to bringing her onto our *Beach Getaway* set, to meet all my new friends and acquaintances and see this strange world her daughter had blundered into. Most of all, I was excited by the prospect of introducing her to Tommy. What would they make of each other? They seemed to be from two different worlds, my own two alternate universes, and I hoped that seeing them together would clarify some things for me.

I had a difficult decision to make pretty soon. Several times Tommy had offered to introduce me to his agent. "Samantha knows all about you and she really wants to meet you. She's sure she can get you TV work, and maybe another movie." Also, Arvy had begun to talk to me about another project he had in preproduction. "You'd be perfect for it," he said. "It's a little bit of a bigger film than *Beach Getaway* and I can't offer you the job right off the bat. But if you want to read for it, we'd sure give you a long and serious look." So as the last days of July slipped toward August, a big decision loomed. Either I would make plans to return to New Jersey to finish high school, or talk to my parents about staying in Los Angeles, finding a school here, and giving Hollywood a real try.

"This looks like any high school, anywhere," Mom

said when we reached the outside of the building. "Except for all the equipment trucks."

"It's supposed to look like a normal high school," I told her. "And those aren't all equipment trucks. Some of them are trailers for the stars."

"You get your own trailer?" Mom seemed genuinely amazed.

"If you're nice to me, I just might let you into it," I told her. "But first, come, I want to introduce you to all the guys."

It was a nice film crew, and they couldn't have treated my mother any better. Jason made her sit in his director's chair while he explained the opening composition of the first shot of the day to her, and Bruce, the cameraman, sent her up in the crane high above the school's gymnasium floor. Jane, the tough-as-nails assistant director, told my mother that of all the actors she had worked with, I was one of the very nicest and best behaved.

"Are you sure you're talking about my daughter?" Mom asked her, feigning disbelief, but I could tell she was very pleased.

"So that's where Liz gets her bluish skin," Anna, the makeup woman, commented when she shook my mother's hand.

"I beg your pardon."

"Your skin is even bluer than your daughter's," Anna said. "It's unusual, and very striking. I bet you take dynamite photographs. Have you ever worked in front of a camera?"

"I did some print modeling years ago," Mom told her.

That completely surprised me. Mom had never mentioned anything about modeling. "When?" I asked her. "What kind of modeling?"

She shrugged it off. "Just silly stuff, when I was your age, and a little more in college. I didn't have much money and it helped pay the bills."

"Do you still have any of the pictures?"

"I tried to destroy all the available copies. To tell you the truth, I didn't like doing it."

Tommy's call time was about an hour after mine, so my mom had already met just about everybody else in the cast and crew when he sauntered onto the set in his usual blue jeans and a T-shirt. He looked as handsome, relaxed, and confident as ever. "Mom," I said, nodding in his direction as he approached, "here comes Tommy, my hunk of a costar."

She turned to look, and they saw each other at exactly the same time. Tommy smiled one of his fourteen-karat smiles. My mom smiled back one of her own. He walked over and held out his right hand and, before I could even make an introduction he said, "I'm Tommy Fletcher, Mrs. Wheaton. It's a real honor meeting you." As if slipping instinctively into a new role, Tommy seemed a little bit more serious, formal, and dignified than I had ever seen him before. Even his choice of conversation seemed uncharacteristically cautious and polite. "Did you have a good flight out?"

"Yes, thank you."

"If you have questions about anything on the set, or about the moviemaking process, or if you need anything to eat or drink, please ask me. I've been doing this a long time and I want you to be my guest here."

"That's very kind of you," Mom said. "And thank you for taking such good care of my Lizzy."

Tommy glanced at me — I guess he was wondering what I had told my mother about him and what she meant by her remark. I shrugged slightly and looked away. Tommy saw he wasn't going to get any help from my direction. "She doesn't need taking care of," he finally replied, shooting my mom a trademark grin. "When I first met her, I kinda wondered where someone that young, from a small town, learned to be so polished and classy, not to mention smart and beautiful. But now that I've met her mother, it's obvious."

Mom laughed. "If you can come up with lines like that on your own, I don't know why they even bother writing scripts for you."

"The truest lines come out the best," Tommy said with a tiny grin and an improbable mixture of quiet sincerity and self-mocking playfulness. "Now, if you'll excuse me, I have to go get ready for my first shot."

He walked away and Mom turned to me. "So that's your new friend?"

I couldn't decipher the amused expression on her face. "He's a terrific actor," I replied, a little nervously.

"How can you tell?"

When you can't understand what your mother is saying, but you know she's gently making fun of you, sometimes the best thing to do is to retreat. "I also better go get my final touch-up. It looks like they're just about ready to walk through my first shot."

"Go get some more makeup on that bluish skin," Mom said, waving me away. "I'm looking forward to seeing you in the spotlight."

Mom got her wish many times over that week, as we did a number of hilarious scenes in which I was either the star or split the lines with Tommy. In the school's gymnasium scene, my character left a volleyball game and snuck out of the locker room through a window, managing to hit her head and get most of her clothes caught in the process. Later, we did the cafeteria scene where Tommy and I meet for the first time, and our back-and-forth repartee about my putting catsup on a taco was so funny that the crew members were all chuckling between takes.

My mother was fascinated by the whole process. She asked questions and was taken here and there around the set, and by the end of the week seemed to know just about everyone in the crew and cast.

In the evenings, Peg, Mom, and I gallivanted around Los Angeles, shopping, eating great meals, and having all sorts of adventures. Peg seemed determined to prove to us that Los Angeles had it all, from a symphony orchestra, to comedy clubs, to experimental theater where an almost-nude couple screamed insults at each other that were supposed to be incisive but mostly sounded just plain stupid, to a poetry reading at the Getty Art Museum, which was built on a hillside in Malibu as an exact replica of a Roman temple.

I got a kick out of hearing them tease each other about men and clothes and whatever entertainment Peg had chosen for us that particular evening. My mom had changed a lot since the days when they were footloose and fancy-free college students together. She seemed to enjoy this week-long chance to slip back into a mind-set of nearly twenty years past. Peg, at least according to my mother, hadn't changed one bit. In fact, there were accusations that she had actually gotten worse.

A lot of the discussions and good-natured teasing had to do with Peg's dilemma about Arthur. She had promised him a response by the end of the summer, and she swung one way and then the other from day to day. "Of course he's not perfect," my mother admonished her again and again. "Of course he doesn't meet all of your requirements. You're in love with a mental image, not a real man. You'll never find what you're looking for, but you have found a great guy and you'd better grab him before somebody else does." Peg laughed at my mother's seriousness, but I could see that she also listened.

The week flew by. My only regret was that Tommy seemed unusually busy and had to turn down my almost daily invitations to get together with us in the evenings. The last day of my mother's visit I had hoped that he could join us for dinner, but he apologized and explained that he had an evening meeting with a very exclusive personal manager that he just couldn't afford to pass up. "Anyway," he said, "I'm sure the two of you have lots to talk about on your mother's last evening. It was a pleasure meeting you, Mrs. W. I thought I was in love with Lizzy, but now I think maybe I'm in love with her mother."

"You're a truly gifted actor," my mom told him with a laugh. "And I'm going to spend the rest of my life watching you star in movies."

"Hopefully I'll be starring in some of them with your daughter," Tommy said, kissed her good-bye on the side of the cheek, and walked away.

When we were done shooting on that last afternoon of her visit, Mom and I wandered off by ourselves. Peg was busy that evening, and I was secretly grateful for the chance to keep my mom all to myself. People in Los Angeles don't seem to like to walk, but Mom can hike for hours and I like walking, too. We headed north, and eventually came to a fashionable stretch of Montana Avenue with chic boutiques and dance studios and clothing stores for children.

We found a cute little restaurant with a trendy-sounding name that served food from all different countries, all mixed together. Soon we were seated at a table, splitting a goat cheese-and-shitake mushroom pizza as our appetizer. I noticed that a lot of the other people in the restaurant were eating their pizza with a knife and fork, but we ate ours East Coast style — with our hands. "You know, Liz," my mom said, finishing off a triangle of whole wheat pizza crust, "I'm not just saying this because I'm your mother — you really are very, very good at movie acting."

"I've been working at it pretty hard, and taking lessons."

"A talent is a talent. I was amazed to watch you on the set all week. You absolutely deserve to be one of the stars. And movie stars are famous for leading very comfortable and glamorous lives." She finished her last slice and a waiter took the pizza tray away. "You've already earned more money this summer than I make in a whole year teaching English," she said, as if the fact bemused her.

I swallowed the last piece of my own pizza and nodded. It seemed crazy that I could make more than her so quickly and easily. Mom had been teaching for twelve years. "That seems very unfair. I mean, you work hard and you're really good at what you do."

"The rewards of a teaching career are not monetary," Mom said. "And I can't complain — your father and I are doing okay. You on the other hand" — she smiled and jabbed toward me through the air with the tines of her fork — "are moving into what business-people call a high-end profession. There's no upper limit. And there's a reason for that. Very few people look the way you do and can do what you do in front of a camera." She hesitated, and I sort of knew what was coming. "Which raises the question of do you want to give it all up and come home at the end of the summer?"

Soft classical music played through the restaurant. The main courses arrived, giving me a few more seconds to figure out how to begin to answer her question.

I had fettucini with bits of crispy Chinese duck, sun-dried tomatoes, and a creamy sauce. Mom had a skinless breast of chicken in a vodka-orange marinade, with peapods and baby carrots on the side.

A giant mirror completely covered one large wall, and in its reflection I could see a mother and a daughter having what looked like a nice, relaxed, and normal dinner. I swallowed my first forkful of fettucini and then took a deep breath. "Tommy has offered to introduce me to his agent. She's done a great job with his career, and she thinks she can get me TV work. Also, Arvy, that producer . . ."

"I remember Arvy and his sidekick, Harold, very well," my mom said with a rueful smile.

"They think I may be right for another project they have. It would be an even bigger role."

It was my mother's turn to let some time pass. She nodded, and seemed to be slicing her breast of chicken with unusual concentration. "Your father and I have discussed this," she finally said in a low voice. "We want to support you, whatever your decision is. Naturally we'd love you to come home." She looked up from her plate at me. "We worry about you here. And, of course, we can't just sell the house, quit our jobs, and move to California. But there are a couple of different ways we could try to work things out. The big question is, is this really what you want to do?"

"I don't know," I admitted. "I really, really, don't know."

"Do you enjoy the lifestyle?"

"Yes, a lot of the time." I hesitated. "This is going to sound really bad. . . ."

"Fire away," Mom said.

"It's nice to be a star," I told her. "And to be treated like one. When I want ice water on the set, someone brings it to me. When I want a wardrobe change, it's ready. I can get a makeup touch-up or my nails done or my hair fixed any time I want. I get my own trailer. The other day some strangers came to our set and waited an hour for me to sign autographs. You should have seen the way they were looking at me. Like I was some kind of . . ."

"Big Hollywood star," my mom suggested.

I nodded. "And it's not only that. The people are

fascinating . . . Inge Mannheim is one of a kind. Jason is a brilliant director. And Tommy . . ." I didn't know how to finish.

"Is a talented, colorful young man," Mom said, helping me.

"You don't like him, do you?"

"I don't know him," she said. "I just hope you do." For a long moment we looked into each other's faces, and the music and chatter in the restaurant seemed to dwindle away till it was just the two of us, all alone. I tried to read something in her eyes, and I think she tried to read something in mine. Finally Mom smiled. "Let's finish this dinner and get back to the soap opera of Peg's life."

After dinner, we walked home together through the dark and empty Santa Monica streets. It's strange considering the number of young and energetic people who live in that area, but almost nobody was out walking. In the Jersey suburbs when Mom and I would go out for a walk we would always pass somebody we knew. But in Santa Monica, it seemed like the sidewalks had been made just for us.

"You did a pretty good job in the restaurant explaining why you might want to stay here," my mother said. "Anybody would want to be a star. What makes you want to come home?"

"Two goofy parents," I told her.

"There must be a better reason than that."

I had been thinking about it off and on for several weeks, and when I tried to answer, things just started spilling out. "A boyfriend who doesn't play the French horn all that great. Thunderstorms and snow days off from high school. My friends . . . and an old house with a basement and an attic that makes strange noises when the wind blows. Neighbors nodding to each other in the streets, and trees, real trees that have branches and roots . . . I don't know, maybe I can't explain it. . . ." I looked at her. "Tommy's introduced me to a few TV and movie stars my age or a little older who make hundreds of thousands of dollars a year. Even if I could, I don't know if I'm ready to make that much money. I think making that much money can change a person's personality. Does that make any sense?"

"Keep talking," Mom said.

"I don't know if I'm ready to have that much wild fun and constant excitement. It feels like a permanent vacation."

"There's nothing wrong with making money and having fun, as long as the compass needle points to north," my mother said, repeating the expression I had heard her use on her first day in Los Angeles, when we had walked down Venice Beach.

We reached Peg's block and I slowed down. This conversation was important to me. I had to find a way to ask Mom a question that I didn't know how to phrase. "Peg told me that when you were in college, you dated a zillionaire."

She looked surprised and even a little angry. "Peg talks too much sometimes."

"She said the zillionaire wanted to marry you. And that he was very handsome."

Mom stopped walking. We were about fifty feet from Peg's building, standing beneath a eucalyptus tree, half in streetlight and half in shadow. "I don't think your Aunt Peg has ever forgiven me for not marrying that fellow from Chicago," Mom said. "She would have, in a minute. Most of my college friends told me I was crazy. I could have had anything. Clothes. Travel. He used to shower me with ridiculously expensive furs and jewelry."

"Do you ever regret it?" I whispered. "I mean, I know that you and Dad are happy. But do you ever think back on it?"

She put her hands lightly on my shoulders and we looked into each other's faces. "Do you know what the ancient Greeks used to say was the key to happiness?"

I shook my head.

"Know thyself," she told me. "I think they were right. Everybody has a different formula for happiness and fulfillment. In my case, it was a high school teacher who makes bad puns and smokes a pipe. And, no, I've never regretted it." She glanced up at the white condominium fifty feet down the street and frowned, as if seeing something that disturbed her. "In Peg's case, I don't think she's ever known what she really wanted. So even though she could've had anything and any man when she was young, and she still can, she hasn't led a happy life. And I'm afraid she's going to screw it up again." She lowered her eyes to mine. "In your case, Liz . . ."

"Tell me," I begged her in a whisper.

"Do you expect mothers to have any special wisdom?"

I nodded. "If not, what are they good for?"

That got a little smile. We looked at each other. "I can't believe I'm almost forty," she finally whispered. "Life goes by so very, very quickly. Three or four times you come to crossroads."

I nodded. "I feel that."

"Don't try to look away down the roads. Instead, look deep inside yourself. Figure out what really makes you tick. Is it, for example, a handsome and charming young man?" She smiled at me, a suspicious and at the same time strangely knowing little smile. "There's absolutely nothing wrong with handsome young men, Liz."

I didn't say anything. The street was dark and quiet.

"Is it wealth?" she continued. "For some people, money makes the world go 'round. Is it fame? You have to decide for yourself. No one else can do it for you, from the outside, no matter how much they love you."

Her voice took on a warning tone. "And don't you ever let anyone else do it for you. If they try to, push them away. Once you decide what you really want, then and only then look down the roads. And once you've chosen, if you look back, you'll just be wasting your time." She took a breath. "Enough advice for one night. We'd better go see if Peg has given Arthur his walking papers yet."

So we started walking again, slowly, matching each other step for step. "You don't think she'll marry him?" I asked.

"He would make her too happy," Mom said, shaking her head sadly. "It's a terrible thing to have to say, but people who spend their lives in search of perfection really and truly must love to suffer." And then she took my hand, and led me out of the shadows toward Peg's white condominium.

CHAPTER 20

Tommy wasn't much good at apologizing, but as the elevator rose into the upper reaches of a Century City high-rise, he was trying his best. "I really wanted to spend time with you and your mother," he said. "She was great. It was just a bad week for me."

"I guess I was hurt that you couldn't even manage one evening," I told him.

It was a mirrored elevator, so we could see ourselves in all four walls. I was dressed up for the coming interview, and Tommy was dressed down. "Lizzy, things just kept coming up. I have hot weeks and cold weeks. If you don't believe me, ask Samantha when you meet her."

"I believe you. It's just that . . . Mom was here for a whole week. And except meeting her on the set, when you had no choice, you didn't spend a minute with us."

"So shoot me," he said, starting to sound a little

angry himself. He put his hands into the pockets of his jeans and looked at me intently. Seconds ticked by. As we flew past the thirtieth floor, he added in a low voice, "Look . . . maybe because I don't have a family of my own, sometimes it's hard for me to spend time with other people's mothers and fathers. If that's a character flaw, shoot me."

I was trying to think of what to say when the thirty-fifth floor light blinked and the doors opened. Tommy walked out and I followed. How could I have expected someone whose parents had died in a car accident fairly recently to spend time laughing and having a good time with my mother? How could I have been so tremendously selfish?

"Stop looking so glum," Tommy commanded as receptionists waved us on down glistening marble corridors and bestowed brilliant smiles on Tommy. "I brought you here for a reason. In Hollywood, the road to fame and fortune detours behind the agents' desks. So look alive, baby."

It must have been an interesting place to work. We passed chic receptionists, young agents-in-training who looked like frat boys and sorority girls, thirtyish fast-track yuppy agents in small offices with phones pressed to their ears, and elegantly attired senior-management types in corner suites with floor-to-ceiling windows. The place positively hummed with energy— it reminded me of a giant beehive. And from the snippets of conversations we overheard as we hurried past, it sounded like this beehive manufactured money rather than honey.

Samantha Wong was clearly a queen bee. She was a short, elegant Chinese woman in her forties, resplendent in a blue silk dress with a high neckline. Her black hair was done up theatrically in a waterfall of curls and tresses, and an enormous ruby ring on one of her fingers glittered in the sunlight that poured into her corner suite. She stood up as we entered, smiled, and hurried around her desk to greet us. I thought to myself that Inge Mannheim would approve of the way Samantha Wong walked — she carried herself with poise and grace.

She shook my hand and kissed Tommy on the lips, and in twenty seconds we were all sitting on leather chairs near the west windows of her office. A young assistant came in and asked us what we'd like to drink. Tommy had a Coke. I asked for a Sprite. Samantha Wong had a glass of herbal tea.

We made small talk for a few minutes. Samantha had grown up in New York and passed through Leonia. She asked me how the schools were there and what my parents did. Tommy kept quiet, sipping his Coke and listening to the two of us chat.

Finally, Samantha came to the point. "Tommy's told me a little bit of how you found your way to Hollywood. When it comes to beauty and talent, Hollywood has a sharp eye and a long arm. Tell me, do you have representation now?"

"You mean an agent? No."

"Who looked over your contracts for *Beach Getaway*?"

"My dad's lawyer, in New Jersey."

"Do you have any photographs?"

"Professional ones, for sending out?"

"That's right. Head shots."

"No," I said. "Some of the guys on the set of *Beach Getaway* have been offering to introduce me to photographers who do that. But I haven't yet."

"Good," Samantha Wong said. "Because you don't want to have your shots taken by somebody's friend. You want the very best. Those photographs will be your business cards and your preliminary auditions, rolled into one. Are you familiar with Shannon Dune?"

"No," I said.

Samantha looked very slightly perturbed.

"Lizzy's an East-Coast snob," Tommy told her. "She doesn't watch much TV." Then he explained to me, "Shannon Dune's a TV actress, about your age. Samantha's built her career into a success in just a couple of years."

"Seventeen months," Samantha said. "When she walked through that door, she had less on her résumé than you do, Elizabeth. Now she's a legitimate young star. She recurs on a network series. She's worked in daytime soaps. And she's had several small but good movie roles. She will probably make half a million dollars this year."

"That's very impressive," I said.

Samantha Wong sipped her herbal tea. "I could do the same for you. Would you be interested in signing with my agency?"

"To tell you the truth . . ." I paused and took a deep breath. "I don't know if I'm going to be staying in Hollywood. But if I do, I'd love to work with your agency."

Samantha Wong glanced at Tommy.

"Liz keeps pretending that she might go back to New Jersey and finish high school," he told her. "And then she might go on to college and become a veterinarian."

Samantha's perfectly lined and plucked eyebrows lifted very slightly.

"It's a tough decision," I told her, sounding to myself as if I were apologizing for even hesitating to take her up on her offer. "I have to make it in the next week."

I guess she heard the strain in my voice. She studied me for a moment, and sympathy showed clearly in her elegant face. "I remember when I left the nest for the first time," she said. "I was scared stiff. Whether it's for a movie career at sixteen or college at eighteen, it's never easy, Elizabeth. But opportunity doesn't always knock twice." Suddenly there was a serious and cautionary tone in her voice. "Sometimes it only knocks once." She folded her fingers into a tiny fist and rapped on the glass coffee table.

"Sounds like it's knocking right now," Tommy told me. "Do you hear it?"

"Yes," I admitted. "I do."

"A one in ten thousand opportunity," Samantha said. "That's a pretty important knock. Thousands of girls come here from all over the country, from all over the whole world — pretty, talented, and very, very determined. Maybe one makes it into the big time. One out of ten or fifteen thousand." She smiled at me. "How very lucky to be the one named Elizabeth Wheaton."

"I really, really appreciate what you're offering me."

"Do you?" she asked. "I wonder . . . ?" We looked at each other for several seconds in silence. Finally, she glanced at her watch. "I'm afraid I have another meeting in three or four minutes, so let me come straight to the point." She leaned slightly forward.

"People I respect tell me you're a natural actor. You have a great, very fresh look. And everyone seems to like you, which is rare in this town. We could do well together. I never, never say this, but I'm saying it to you — I want you as a client."

I didn't know what to say. "Thank you," I heard myself whisper. My whole body was buzzing . . .

something about her complete confidence and enthusiasm for my future career prospects was getting to me, pumping me up with so much adrenaline that I could barely stay in my seat. It seemed like she was offering me a golden key to the future. I would be crazy to even hesitate.

"Don't thank me. It would be to both of our benefits. I happen to know of a project you'd be perfect for. A wonderful part, a major role . . . and it would just be the beginning. So you think it over. Talk to Tommy and your parents. And call me within a week." She stood, and I stood also. "Hopefully we'll be seeing a lot of each other."

"Yes. I hope so, too. Thanks for everything," I mumbled, my hand actually shaking.

On the elevator heading down to the street, I thanked Tommy for introducing me to his agent. "I know that's a big favor. And I could tell that she's a really important woman."

"I was doing her a favor, too," Tommy said. "She talked to Jason and Inge Mannheim, and they must have told her very positive things. And I said a few nice things about you myself."

The elevator door opened and we walked out of the building into the afternoon sunlight. In the courtyard beneath the high-rise, a stone fountain sent streams of water gushing upward. Well-dressed lawyers and executives sat on benches around the fountain. "So, tell me you're gonna sign with her?" Tommy asked me.

"I'm real tempted."

"But you're still not sure?" He stopped in front of the fountain, took a penny out of his pocket, and put it on his palm. "I'm gonna make a wish." He closed his eyes and flipped the copper disc up into the sunlight. It landed in the middle of the fountain. "Want to know what I wished for?"

"If you tell, it won't come true."

"I wished that you could understand what people have been trying to tell you, Liz. It doesn't seem to completely get through. Do you want me to try, once more, or not?"

"Go ahead."

"You remember all those boys in your high school who didn't even know you, but asked you to the prom? And it made you uncomfortable."

I nodded.

"That happened for a reason," Tommy told me. "You don't belong there. You're too pretty for there. You're too talented for there. If the shoe doesn't fit, don't try to wear it. You belong here. With me. In this world. This is what God gave you, Lizzy. Do you know what I'm saying?"

I nodded and felt a little frightened because his words had the ring of truth.

"God didn't make you an opera singer. He didn't make me tall enough to be a pro basketball player. Instead, he made us both physically beautiful and gave us acting talent." Tommy turned away from the fountain to look at me. He put his hands on my shoulders and looked right into my eyes, as if trying to hypnotize me. "Samantha gave it to you straight — ten thousand girls do come to Hollywood for every one who succeeds. And you didn't even want to come, but the long arm of Hollywood reached out and grabbed you. Now important agents are turning cartwheels to get you to stay. This is your destiny. And know what?"

"What?"

"It's not such a bad destiny. This world can be a lot more fun and creative than you think. You've worked in Hollywood, but you haven't experienced how it is at the top. I mean, at the very top, which is where we're both headed. Would you like to?"

"When?"

"Tonight," he said. "Last time we went slumming. Tonight, we blast off into orbit. Are you game?"

"As long as we won't have to sneak in anywhere."

"We won't," Tommy promised, smiling. "That's a girl. By the end of this evening, you'll know what it's like to be a star in heaven on earth." He kissed me gently on the lips. "'Cause like it or not, that, baby, is where you belong."

CHAPTER 21

Tommy showed up at seven-fifteen. He was wearing an elegant black tuxedo and he carried a big white box and a smaller, blue one, under his arm. I had put on my best party dress, and the first thing he said was, "You look great." But then he added, "Liz, I want to try an experiment. Go into your bedroom and slip this on. And take this little box, too."

With his straw-blond hair cascading toward the black velvet lapels, and his powder-blue bow tie matching the bright blue of his eyes, it was hard to look away from Tommy. As I headed for my bedroom, I noticed that Peg couldn't quite manage the trick. Her eyes were sticking to him like there was epoxy glue on his bow tie.

I put the box on my bed and opened it. Inside was a black silk evening gown. The little box held matching black shoes with two-inch heels. I had never told

Tommy my dress or shoe size, but when I took off my old dress and squirmed into the new one, everything fit perfectly. I stood in front of my bedroom's full-length mirror, enraptured.

It was sleek, slinky, and sexy; strapless and very chic. If the neckline had been an inch lower or the hemline a tiny bit higher, it would have been too risqué for me to feel comfortable in. But it managed to be daring yet classy, which is a difficult trick for a dress. And when I walked in it, with the shoes lifting me an inch or so higher than usual above the ground, the dress seemed to have a life and voice of its own, and to whisper, "Smile" to me. "Smile, you look ravishing. This is your night."

When I came out of the bedroom, Peg was still staring at Tommy. My appearance drew both of their attention. Peg's jaw dropped. Tommy's eyes flashed as he came over and took my arm.

"How did you know my size?"

"I've put my arms around you a couple of times. You look very, very beautiful."

"The dress is wonderful. I'll try to take care of it tonight."

"It's yours now. You deserve each other."

"I couldn't possibly accept such an expensive gift."

He glanced at his watch. "We should go. Have a good evening, Peg."

"You, too. Have a good evening," Peg managed to mumble back, still apparently mesmerized by this vision in a black tux. She walked us to the door. "Enjoy your-self, Liz," she told me, and she couldn't quite keep the envy out of her voice. "This looks to me like one of those nights life was meant to be lived for. Have a ter-rific time."

When Tommy picked me up, I never knew what he would be driving. Sometimes it was his motorcycle. Or a van. Or a car he had borrowed from a friend. Tonight it was a low-slung black Porsche with bucket seats. "This Saudi Arabian guy I know lent it to me," he said. "I figured we should arrive in style."

"Arrive where?"

"I had a small part in a big movie, and tonight is the premiere," he told me. "And you know what that means?"

"Not exactly."

He pressed the gas and the sports car jumped down the block like a hungry panther. "Red carpets and French champagne," he said.

The theater was in Westwood, near UCLA. Even from ten blocks away, it was easy to see that something big was up. Searchlights reached up through the black-ness, crisscrossing on the dark faces of night clouds. A crowd all but blocked the entrance to the theater. Cars honked at each other, valet parkers hustled back and forth, and policemen and bodyguards kept autograph hounds and overly enthusiastic fans behind wooden sawhorses.

Tommy eased the Porsche to a stop in front of the

theater. A bodyguard in a dark suit helped me out and sort of handed me to Tommy, who took my arm and whispered, "Let's make an entrance, Lizzy Bird. Chin up and keep smiling." Then we marched forward, along a red carpet that led into the theater.

"There's Tommy!" a young, female voice called from behind the sawhorses.

"Tommy Fletcher? Where?"

"In that tux! Tommy! LOOK AT HIM! OH! GODDDD!"

Tommy waved to his fans. Security people ushered us in past barriers of red velvet ropes. Suddenly, the night turned into blinding day. Hundreds of flash-bulbs popped in unison as two dozen photographers swarmed toward us. "Smile and keep walking," Tommy whispered, gripping my arm a little tighter.

And then we were by the cameramen, inside the lobby. It looked like a world-class assembly of the beautiful and powerful. Distinguished-looking men in elegant black tie and beautiful women in flowing, fan-tastic, and for the most part super sexy outfits milled around getting free popcorn from concession stands, giving interviews to newsmen, having pictures taken together, and generally making themselves part of the high-energy scene.

I glimpsed five or six world-famous actors and ac-tresses whose movies I had loved for years. Flawlessly dressed and coiffed, they were stars in every sense of the word. Their faces seemed to radiate heat and light, and each of them exerted a different kind of peculiar personal gravity that sucked dozens of admirers into their orbits.

Tommy introduced me to several of them and to a number of other bigwigs whose names I had heard often during the past summer. There were studio presidents and Academy Award winning directors, producers and glamorous models, all smiling and making small talk. I was impressed by how many of them seemed to know Tommy well enough to joke around with him.

We went in and found seats in a middle row. "This is a nervous time for all of us, but especially for the producers," Tommy told me. "This picture cost twenty-five million."

"Twenty-five million dollars?"

"They've tested it on a few audiences before, but how would you like to be sitting there with that kind of money on the line, finding out what jokes clunk and what performances don't work for a live audience?"

In this case, the producers had nothing to worry about. It wasn't a great movie, but it was very good and the audience laughed and bit their nails in all the right places. Tommy had a very small part near the end. He only had a handful of lines but he absolutely nailed them — his only wisecrack got a big laugh. I squeezed his hand to let him know how good he was.

After the movie there was a reception at a Beverly Hills restaurant. "We just need to put in an appearance," Tommy told me. Once again, we floated in on a long and magical red carpet as flashbulbs popped and female fans called to Tommy from behind sawhorses. Inside the trendy nightspot, waiters hurried back and forth with glasses of champagne and fabulous trays of finger food. In the center of the restaurant, on white linen tablecloths, was a seafood dinner buffet that was not to be believed: a mountain of cracked Alaskan crab claws, giant shrimp, five different kinds of oysters, grilled salmon, and vegetables and wild rice.

I followed Tommy's example and ate sparingly. Most of all it was fun just to look around at the rich and famous. I had never known that so many perfect-looking women existed on this whole planet. Their hair, makeup, teeth, hard bodies — all were absolutely flawless. Some of them were with perfect-looking guys, but most of them were on the arms of men who looked old enough to be their fathers. The older men talked. The young women tilted back their heads, and laughed, and sipped champagne.

I don't normally drink, but Tommy had seated us at a table with two other couples, and soon a champagne toast was proposed. I went along with it, clinked glasses, sipped the bubbly liquid, and enjoyed our table conversation. One of the guys we were seated with was a famous young stand-up comic, and he was absolutely hilarious. He started doing impressions, Tommy did some of his own back, and soon our whole table was roaring with laughter. I looked down and realized that a waiter had refilled my glass of champagne without my knowing it. I pushed the glass away and stuck to ice water for the rest of the meal.

The party was just hitting its stride when Tommy excused us and led me away from our table. "Why are we leaving?" I asked. "Did I do something wrong?"

"Don't be silly. That wasn't really the party," he said.

"It was the best party I've ever been to."

"It was nothing. I'm gonna show you a real premiere party."

I dozed in the bucket seat as we purred along in the black Porsche through the empty streets of the Westside. The champagne had made me drowsy. I woke with a jolt as we pulled to an abrupt stop before a long pier. "Wake up, Sleeping Beauty," Tommy told me with a laugh. "We're here."

"Where?"

"Marina del Rey. My buddy Pierre is throwing the 'real' party tonight."

"Who's Pierre?"

"One of the backers of the film. He owns a little boat that he likes to throw exclusive parties on." Tommy helped me out of the bucket seat. Around us, limos and expensive cars were pulling up and a few dozen people whom I recognized from the first party in Beverly Hills were streaming steadily down a long dock.

Tommy and I followed them, past big and small boats. At the very end of the dock, a magnificent yacht was all lit up. The main mast looked like a giant floating Christmas tree, with a forest of brilliantly lighted smaller trees surrounding it. "This is the little boat your friend Pierre owns?" I asked Tommy.

"Not only does he own it, but he knows how to throw a pretty good party on it," Tommy assured me, leading me up the gangplank.

The yacht looked to me to be more than a hundred feet long, with a swimming pool on the rear deck and lots of open space up front. Tables had been set up around a five-piece jazz band, and since the deck was made of wood, it was like one enormous dance floor.

A dashingly handsome, white-haired man in his fifties, immaculate in a white dinner jacket, stood near the gangplank. "Come, meet Pierre," Tommy said, leading me over to him.

Pierre seemed to use our approach to extricate himself from a conversation he had tired of. "Thomas," he shouted, and waved as we got close. His French accent gave his English exotic flair. "So you've arrived and now we can set sail?"

He walked over and kissed Tommy on both cheeks, European-style. Then he gave me a long look.

"This is Elizabeth," Tommy told him. And then to me, "My friend, Pierre, who owns half of Europe."

I had never met a yacht owner before. He had strong features and there was something in his face — particularly about his eyes — that suggested to me that for all his charm Pierre would be a very dangerous man to cross.

"Actually, I only own a quarter of Europe. May I?" Pierre asked, holding out his right hand. I thought he wanted to shake it, so I was a little embarrassed when he said, "No, no, my dear," turned my wrist, raised my fingers to his lips, and kissed the back of my hand. He didn't let go. "Such soft skin," he said. "Elizabeth, I'm afraid I've fallen in love with your hand. May I keep it for a moment?"

I didn't have much practice at making this kind of conversation with European zillionaires. "Sure," I said. "As long as you give it back eventually."

So Pierre kept my hand in his own right hand, looped his left arm around my back, and led Tommy and me along the deck toward the jazz band. "I have always had a weakness for young beauty," he told us. "Tonight, you two are my special guests. If you want anything, anything at all, just ask. Do you sing, Elizabeth?"

"Only in the shower," I told him.

"Then I'm afraid an old man like me will never get to hear it. A shame, so lovely a little bird should have a song. Will you excuse me?" The arm unlooped from behind my back, my right hand was released, and suddenly Pierre was hurrying back down the deck to welcome a fat man who was arriving with a girl who looked younger than me on his arm.

We cast off, the jazz band began to play, and people waved and called out to us from docks and other boats as we cruised by. "Hey, great music!" "Have a good one!" "Can we come?"

It wasn't a very big party, compared to the one in Beverly Hills. There couldn't have been more than fifty guests, and the big deck accommodated them easily. I noticed that many of the most beautiful and famous people from the restaurant had found their way onto Pierre's yacht.

The temperature was warm — almost balmy — and there was a steady ocean breeze to keep us cool. In the dark sky above, a regally full moon sat high on a throne of stars. The yacht made good time and soon we left the marina behind and sailed out into the open Pacific. The waves got noticeably larger, but the big yacht barely rocked. Soon the whole glittering arc of coastline from Long Beach to Malibu was visible.

I knew enough about jazz to be certain that the band was very, very good. Food and drinks consisted mainly of champagne, caviar, and fresh fruit. At first I didn't want to drink anymore, but Pierre himself brought me a glass. "It's from one of my own vineyards," he told me. "You must try it."

So I took it, and tried a small sip by the rail. Tommy had his arm around me, and it felt good to be standing so close together. Every so often we glanced at each other and both smiled. When he walked away for a moment, I dumped the champagne over the side and had the bartender fill the glass with ginger ale.

Tommy always looked handsome and very confident, but that night, in his elegant tux on a magnificent yacht with a champagne glass in his hand, it was like there was a divine spotlight shining on him. He had never looked better; he had never been funnier, quicker, or more confident — he was on, on, on. I wasn't the only one who noticed it. At least half a dozen women tried to cut in on me, inventing excuses to come up and talk and then flirting shamelessly with him. Tommy was polite to them, and I knew him well enough not to get mad when he flirted back a little bit.

But all evening long, he only seemed to have eyes for me. He would leave other women standing by the rail, take my hand, and lead me away to the dance floor. When we danced, he held me close and looked into my eyes. "You belong here, Liz," he whispered in my ear. "This is heaven on earth, and you're a Hollywood star of the future. This is you."

In the course of the evening we talked to just about all of the guests on board the yacht. Famous movie stars who had won Academy Awards turned out to be warm and friendly in person. They talked about the movie we had just seen, and how great this party was, and asked me about myself and my plans. Studio presidents took off their tux jackets and told bad jokes. Movie directors described books they were interested in optioning and spun anecdotes about far-off places where they had shot movies and had wild adventures.

Around midnight, I began to feel light-headed. The excitement, the few sips of champagne, and the lateness of the hour all combined to make everything seem lost in delicious limbo. The night air was salty on my tongue. Gulls followed our boat — I couldn't always see them but I could hear their hungry cries in stark counterpoint to the jazz.

Tommy and I found our own place to dance on the side of the deck. The music was soft and throbbing. He pressed his strong body up tight against mine and I put my arm around him. "Lizzy Bird," he whispered. "Let me show you the rest of the yacht."

"Why? I love it up here," I told him. But a minute later he was leading me down a spiral wooden staircase. There were three levels below the main deck, and many small and large rooms. A fabulous kitchen. "Pierre's a Frenchman — he likes to eat well," Tommy explained. An elegant dining room. An office with an antique rosewood desk facing a long curved window. Crew bunks. Two guest bedrooms. And then Tommy led me to impressive walnut double doors.

"What's this?" I asked.

He pulled out a key and opened the doors. We stepped inside and he pulled them closed behind us and locked them from the inside. It was a large, wood-paneled master bedroom, with plush carpeting and a beamed ceiling. An enormous circular bed lay next to three portholes that were cracked open to admit the cool night air. Jazz drifted down from the upper deck and filtered in through these small windows. "Kick off those heels," Tommy told me.

I did, and he took off his own shoes and socks. My bare toes sank half an inch into the cool, plush carpet. I curled them and dug them in deep — it was an incredibly sensuous feeling. "Now we can dance, just the two of us," Tommy said, and his voice seemed deeper and thicker than normal.

I shut my eyes and let him waltz me up and back. We kissed. He had bought my dress and I guess he was familiar with its hooks and straps and zippers, because I felt his strong fingers move quickly across my shoulder blades and suddenly the black silk fell to my knees. He lifted me out of it and I stood there, almost naked.

"Lizzy," he said, his eyes shining, his hands strong and warm. "Lizzy."

I pulled back after a few seconds.

"Where are you going, Lizzy?"

"Back . . . upstairs . . ."

"You belong here," he whispered. "This is you. Don't fight it." And the perfect blue eyes shone brighter and brighter till they were like two lasers, slicing right through me. "I love you. I love you so much." Our slow dance now had a goal — I saw that he was leading me toward the circular bed.

"Tommy . . ."

All of his defenses lowered at once. Suddenly I saw great vulnerability set against a background of boyishness, and real pain — the kind that only comes from loss. "You know what's happened to me. The grief I've suffered. You know how alone I am. I love you. I need you."

There was so much strength and persuasiveness about him that I stopped protesting as he lifted me onto the bed and lowered me very gently to the silk coverlet. But I was amazed at my own strength, too. Because a short time later — it could have been minutes and it could have been hours — I heard myself say, "No," and again, "No, this isn't what I want."

"You don't even know what you want."

"Not now. I'm not ready."

"Women never know what they want."

"No, Tommy. NO." I said it with a force that surprised myself, and maybe all the education guys get these days about date rape had an effect, too, because Tommy finally pulled back and we lay together, with the sides of our chests touching, listening to the jazz on the giant yacht in Santa Monica Bay.

CHAPTER 22

It was after three in the morning when I slowly climbed the stairs to Peg's apartment. As I fumbled with my key in the lock, I was surprised to see through the window that there was a light on inside. Peg was still awake. I felt disappointed — I very much wanted to be alone with my thoughts, which were running fast and out of control. The champagne glow was wearing off, and I kept replaying different scenes from the long night in my mind.

The Porsche. The Beverly Hills party. The yacht. Pierre and his champagne. The master bedroom.

The key finally turned and the door opened. I stepped inside and saw Peg, sitting on the couch, crying into a Kleenex. Wadded-up yellow tissues were piled on the coffee table and scattered around the floor at her feet. She had clearly been crying for some time. She looked up as I entered, and she tried to smile. Her eyes were red, and her feeble attempt at a smile was a bit horrible to see. "Hi," she said. "How was your party?"

"Fine," I replied, hurrying over to her. "What's wrong?"

"Oh, nothing."

"That's not the way it looks."

Peg followed my gaze down to the wadded-up tissues all over the floor and kicked them into a little pile with her feet. She picked up the pile, carried it over to a trash bin, and tossed it. Then she returned to the couch, looked at me, and sniffled. "Really, Liz, nothing. It's just that I did something tonight that I've been putting off for a long time. I'm sure it was the right thing, so I don't know why I'm carrying on like this . . . except . . . he really was a good man."

"Arthur?"

She touched a yellow Kleenex to her eye. "It was so . . . very difficult to do. But he just wasn't right for me. We would have made each other miserable. I would have tried to change him. He would have tried to change for me." She lowered the Kleenex and looked at me. "People can't change and they shouldn't be made to try. Ultimately it would have ended in bitterness and anger."

I sat down next to her, and stroked her hair. "Well, if you know that, why are you so upset?"

"Because I'm a fool." She tried to smile again. This time she did a little better. "Where was the big bash?"

"On a yacht."

"See, Arthur would never take me to a party on a yacht," she said. "Never in a million years. I know this is going to sound strange, but seeing you and Tommy tonight . . . seeing him in his tux when he came to pick you up . . . with that long hair . . . and the blue bow tie . . . made it all crystal clear for me."

I stopped stroking her hair. "What are you talking about?"

"The way you look at each other," she said. "That electricity. That's the kind of thing I want. That's the kind of charge I need from a relationship. I guess I'll just have to keep looking."

I felt very sorry for her as I stood up, heard myself mumble, "I'm sure you'll find what you're looking for, Peg," and headed off into my bedroom. Even through my closed door I could hear occasional sniffles and sobs. I guess Peg's grip on reality was just strong enough so that she knew, deep down, she had let go of something valuable and hard to find.

I lay awake for a long time.

I had three more days to decide whether to stay in Los Angeles and try to work in Hollywood, or to disappoint Arvy, Samantha Wong, and Tommy Fletcher by returning to New Jersey.

He had told me he loved me. That one magical second from the whole wild whirl of a night stuck fast in my memory. It was the first time a boy had said that to me. Not really a boy — Eric was still in many ways a boy, but Tommy was a man. How his blue eyes had glowed when he said it!

Lying in bed, I was glad I had stopped him when I had, and I also regretted it. My body still tingled from his touch. I still heard his hot whispers in my ear. "You belong here, Liz. I need you. I love you. We were made for each other. We have the talent. We have the looks. We're one in ten thousand. We belong together."

Maybe we were. Maybe I was being insane. Or childish — running home, as Tommy had put it, to my mommy and daddy. Maybe he was one man in ten thousand, and I would never meet anyone like him ever again. I tossed and turned, threw the pillow on the floor and cracked a window open wider, but still sleep would not come. And as I wrestled with these doubts and dilemmas, I heard occasional sniffles and sobs from poor Peg outside in the living room.

CHAPTER 23

The final day of shooting was overcast. We had returned to the beach where we had done most of our shooting to pick up three or four shots that the editors felt they needed in order to cut the film seamlessly. The cloudiness of the day was slowing us down — the director of photography had to match the lighting in these pickup shots as closely as he could with the lighting on the sunny July days when we had done our initial beach shooting.

Nearly everyone on the set felt joy mixed with nostalgia. Our joy came from a sense of accomplishment at having finished a movie, on time and under budget, that our producers were very happy with. We felt nostalgia because over the weeks of shooting together at all times of day and night under all sorts of conditions we had gotten to be pretty close, and after this final afternoon of *Beach Getaway* we knew we would all go off in different directions.

Anna had a job doing makeup on a horror film in a small town in Maine. "It's low-budget shlock, but for a makeup person it's a great opportunity. The gruesomer they want their characters to look, the more of a challenge it is for me," she explained. "I get to be very creative, and one job like this leads to others."

Bruce, the cameraman, was heading to the Philippines to shoot a kick boxer movie.

Jane, our fierce assistant director, was taking a little time off to produce and direct a play in a tiny theater on Melrose Avenue. "I love live theater," she told me. "I just work in movies so that I can make enough money to feed my passion for the stage. We're going to do an original two-act in a ninety-nine-seat Equity waiver theater, and if it's a hit we'll move to a bigger space. If we get killed in the reviews, or ignored, which is just as bad, I'll probably do another movie in a few months."

Jason seemed to have several other projects lined up. The whisper around the set was that a studio wanted him to direct a much bigger budget film, but he refused to talk about his next project too specifically until he was finished with this present one. And as we hurried beneath the thick cloud cover in the late afternoon at the beach, he was having fits about the slowness of the pace. "We're losing light," I heard him mutter to Jane. "And we need to get those last three setups."

Jane took the hint and began bellowing at anyone and everyone, creating a sense of urgency that made everyone work at double and even triple speed.

I don't like working under intense time pressure, so I was glad that I had finished all my shots. There's nothing as tense as a film set when light starts fading and there are still a bunch of shots to get in.

I had planned to have dinner with Tommy that night. We needed to talk about a lot of things, from my plans for the fall to our relationship and what had happened on the yacht. But he was in two of the last three setups so I knew it might be several hours till he was finished. I really didn't want to hang around a tense set that long.

"Get out of this madhouse," Tommy advised me, pausing on his way for a costume change. "Go to Westwood and hang out at my place. Take a nap — try out the futon." He winked at me, and I wondered if he was setting me up for a replay of our time together in the master bedroom of the yacht. "I'll be there in less than two hours. We'll go grab a good dinner and relax." He pressed his key into my hand, gave my wrist a squeeze, and then Jane started shouting for him.

I went for a walk down the beach. It was a strange afternoon — the water appeared a chalky-green color. The clouds completely screened the sun, so that it was hard to tell just how low the sinking sun had gotten. In the distance I could hear Jane shouting, "WE'RE

GOING TO TAKE THIS SHOT IN TWO MIN-UTES! GET FLETCHER. HE CAN FINISH DOING HIS BUTTONS UP DURING CAMERA REHEARSAL. C'MON EVERYBODY, MOVE YOUR BUTTS!"

It sounded like sheer hell, with everyone racing around trying to do their job under time pressure. I knew that I would get to see all the cast and crew members again at the wrap party, when everyone would be in a much more relaxed mood. Right now, it seemed like a good time to take Tommy's advice and escape.

I splurged and took a cab to Westwood. It felt strange to be letting myself into Tommy's apartment without him being there, but it had been his idea. And if he had an ulterior motive for suggesting that I go to his place to wait, I admitted to myself that I had a se-cret reason for taking him up on his offer. It would give me a chance to do a little spying. Not that I was plan-ning to read his diaries or his letters or go through his drawers looking for photos of other girls, but I thought that being in his apartment with some time to look around might give me a better sense of who he was.

I could've saved myself the trouble. A trained secret agent couldn't have unearthed many clues in that apartment. Except for the sports trophies, there were almost no clues to his past. No high school yearbooks. No photographs of friends or family members. Nothing except the furniture, a pretty amazing CD collection, a shelf of paperback best-sellers, and a dozen or so magazines.

So I turned on the TV and watched some stupid comedy till I got really bored. Tommy was right about me being an East Coast snob when it comes to TV — I often have trouble watching sitcoms for more than about ten or fifteen minutes. The jokes just don't seem that funny. I was just getting myself a glass of juice when the doorbell rang.

I figured it was Tommy, home early, but when I opened the door I saw a plump woman in her mid forties standing there, looking a little surprised to see me. "Excuse me," she said, "I thought Tommy Fletcher lived here."

"He does," I told her. "Are you a friend of his?"

"No, but you must be," she said. "I'm Tommy's mother." She held out her hand. "Mary Fletcher."

I backed away from her. You hear a lot of horror stories on movie sets about crazy fans who persuade themselves that they have some kind of close relationship with a star and then stalk them. Because of all of his TV work, Tommy got lots of strange letters from all across America. I figured that what we had here was a first-class loon.

She must have seen the shock in my face, because she lowered her hand and asked, "What's wrong, dear?"

I stood there, frozen, studying her face. Her eyes were light blue and her facial features were very striking. I told myself that there had to be some logical explanation; perhaps her physical resemblance to Tommy had made her develop this delusion that she was his mother.

"You have the strangest look on your face. Please, dear, what's wrong?"

"Tommy Fletcher doesn't have a mother."

It was her turn to look a little surprised. "Everyone has a mother. It's hard to be born without one."

"Tommy's mother was killed two years ago."

"Who told you that?"

"He did. Both his parents were killed in a car accident in Euclid, Ohio."

"We did have a car accident there, but it was little more than a fender bender. Tommy's father is right as rain in Oak Hills. He plays eighteen holes of golf three times a week." She gave an embarrassed laugh. "Don't look so surprised. My Tommy's a good boy at heart, but if you're his friend you should know that you can't believe a word out of his mouth."

"But . . ." I heard myself start and stop. "But . . . why would he lie about a thing like that?"

She shrugged. "It's part of his image. He plays the strong, independent male. He doesn't like us to come around when he's working. . . . I haven't actually seen this apartment since he moved in. But I happened to be in Los Angeles today and I thought I'd find my way out here and surprise him."

"I'm sure you will," I told her. "There's one thing I still don't understand. Even if Tommy likes to play the strong, independent male and all that, how can you let him live so far away from you and have so little contact with you when he's just a year or two out of high school?"

"Twenty-four is plenty old enough to live away from home in my book," she said, then turned away from me with a sudden big smile and opened her arms to embrace her son.

There Tommy was. He froze for a moment when he saw me there, talking to his mother. Our eyes met. He opened his mouth so speak.

I turned around and walked away from him. Down the stairs. Out the gate. Soon I was running. Down the hills of Westwood. My hair flew in the slight breeze. Cars honked at me as I sped through intersections, but I didn't care. Two or three times I heard Tommy's voice calling me, but instead of stopping I just redoubled my speed.

A mile or so from his apartment, I reached the campus of UCLA. Without knowing where I was running or what I was doing, I entered the landscaped campus and began running through the athletic fields.

When I was in the middle of the soccer field, I heard footsteps. I turned and there he was, less than ten feet behind me. He was breathing almost as hard as I was — maybe the athletic trophies were fakes and the story about two hundred sit-ups a day had been a lie also.

"Lizzy," he said. "I see you met my mother. I guess it was a pretty big surprise." He gave me his million-dollar smile.

I felt myself start to cry and I hated that weakness, but there was nothing I could do about it.

He came closer, to comfort me. "Don't touch me," I growled. The anger in my tone made him wary.

"Calm down," he urged. "I admit I told a few fibs, but they don't change anything between us. I still love you."

"How can I believe anything you say?"

"Sometimes I push the truth a little bit, but you can believe this — I never, never do anything that will hurt anyone."

"You hurt me."

"How could my lying about not having parents hurt you? That's crazy."

He stepped forward and I shoved him away with both hands. "It's part of . . . who I thought you were. I've never felt this hurt in my life." My tears had stopped and I found I could look right at him without blinking. "I thought I knew you. I thought I was falling in love with someone I knew. But it was all self-serving lies. That day we went surfing and you made me feel so bad by asking me if I wanted to know how much blood your parents lost in their accident. Lies!" I heard my voice going up, but I didn't even try to control it. "And when my mom visited, and you didn't spend time with us because you said she reminded you of the tragedy you'd been through. And that night on the yacht, when you seemed so vulnerable, and you told me how much grief you'd suffered, and how you loved me. Lies, lies, lies!"

He seemed to get angry himself. "Parents, no parents, accident, no accident . . . Why does it matter?"

"When you pretend to be homeless and eat in a shelter, those are real people you're taking food from. When you lie to me, I'm a real person with real feelings. This isn't just a role in a movie. Don't you understand the difference anymore?" I looked deep, deep into those beautiful blue eyes and saw my answer. "God help you, I actually feel sorry for you."

I tried to walk around him, but he grabbed me. "Lizzy Bird," he said. "You're talking nonsense. We love each other and we're two in twenty thousand. . . ."

I pulled free, slapped him hard on the cheek, and when he let me go I ran off — away from that soccer field.

I'm not sure how I got back to Peg's apartment. I ran and I walked and I caught a bus for a while, and then I ran again. Finally, I found myself just a few blocks from her white condominium and sprinted for home. I took the stairs two at a time, opened the door, hurried into the big, empty apartment, and threw up in the toilet. Then I splashed icy cold water on my face and called home.

Mom answered on the first ring. "Hello?"

"Mom . . ." I took two quick breaths. "It's me."

Maybe it was intuition or maybe from those three words she could tell that something had happened. "What's wrong?" she asked in a very worried voice. "Liz?"

It took me a long time to answer. It felt like I was crying, but there were no tears on my cheeks. Finally I managed to gasp out, "The compass needle's not pointing to north anymore."

"Then come home, baby," she said.

CHAPTER 24

Inge Mannheim was in the middle of a lesson, so I waited outside in the antechamber for nearly twenty minutes. At last a tall, pretty woman in jeans and a black leotard came out of the studio and exited to the street. I watched her leave — she walked gracefully and had perfect posture. I headed through the swinging doors to the large room with the wooden floor and the ceiling fan. The grand old actress was standing in a corner, holding a glass of ice water and swallowing a pill.

"Excuse me for coming by unannounced," I said. "I just wanted to say good-bye and thank you."

She swallowed the pill, washed it down with a big gulp of water, and made a face. "Getting old is no fun," she told me. "But the alternatives are even worse. Now then, Elizabeth, what's all this about good-bye?"

"I've decided to go home and finish high school."

She put down the glass. "I thought you were staying. Samantha Wong has big plans for you."

"I know. She sounded angry when I told her I was leaving." I hesitated. "You were one of the nicest and most interesting people I've met here, and you taught me a lot. I hope you're not disappointed, too."

The sides of her cheeks lifted as she bestowed upon me a big, radiant smile. "Well, aren't you a dear," she said. "I have ten minutes till my next student. Let's sit down and have a chat. Come."

She led me to an inner office that I had never seen before. It was filled with mementos from her long career. One quick glance around at the hundreds of signed photographs on the walls from actors she had taught, or been married to, or worked with, convinced me that Inge had known just about everyone worth knowing since the advent of talking pictures. Particularly the handsome men.

She directed me to a very comfortable chair and sat down opposite me. "So," she said, "you're going back to the provinces?"

"To New Jersey."

"You're turning down fame and bright lights and buckets of money."

"Enough people have already told me I'm crazy."

"If sanity enters into the equation at all, turning down Hollywood can only work in your favor," she said. "In a way, it's quite impressive. What made you decide?"

I shrugged. "I guess . . . it's kind of private." I felt

her wise old eyes on my face and blushed for my last time in Hollywood.

Her face softened. "When a movie shoot ends, leading men and leading ladies often go their separate ways," she told me. "That's part of show business."

"It's not just that. For me Hollywood just isn't a real place. It confuses me. You'll probably laugh at this but . . . if I stay . . . I think it will corrupt me and change me."

"Of course it's not real," she agreed with a laugh. "It's the Emerald City. It's Oz. But that doesn't stop it from being lots of fun. As for corrupting you, Liz dear, I've often thought that every city, like every character in a movie or play, has a unique intention. For example, New York is 'To enliven.' Paris is 'To enthrall.' Venice is 'To make you think deeply.'"

"And Hollywood?" I asked.

"'To seduce,'" she told me without hesitation. "Remember, I came here at seventeen. Innocent and all alone, a beautiful and sleek little kitten from Europe." Her watery eyes were suddenly far away, perhaps picturing herself at seventeen. "Times don't change that much," she finally continued, "even though it may seem like they do. I made my decision to stay, but I certainly understand your decision to leave. And I don't think you'll regret it. Now, I have a lesson in two minutes. . . ." She stood up, and I stood also.

As she led me out of the room with the thousands

of mementos, I couldn't help asking, "Have you ever regretted staying?"

She locked the office door behind us. "Have I?" The question seemed to catch her off guard. "I've had a full, wonderful, magical life. I've been married to three handsome and fascinating men. I've made movies all over the world. I've been to the White House and I've flown a plane and I've shot a tiger." She was silent for just a moment. "If my marriages didn't last and I never managed to have children, that was a price I accepted knowingly. As I have accepted spending my final years alone. We all pay prices. . . ."

Her face quivered. It was suddenly so quiet in the studio room that I could hear the ceiling fan rotating on its brass fittings. Inge Mannheim suddenly drew herself up, and looked positively splendid. "I've never, never regretted it," she said firmly. "Not for one single, solitary moment. I wanted to be a star. I was a star. I am a star. And shallow as it might seem, for sixty years I've had a hoot!"

CHAPTER 25

About half the leaves had fallen off the trees and lay in a colorful carpet along the forest floor. There was a noticeable chill in the air — it was only mid-September but winter was clearly on its way.

Eric and I walked nearly half a mile from the Alpine lookout, till we found a private spot above the Palisades cliffs that looked across the Hudson River at the Manhattan skyline. As we hiked, I told him about my summer *Beach Getaway* experiences, leaving out only a few romantic episodes with Tommy that I thought it might be better to keep to myself.

"I never thought you would come back," he said when I finished. "I would have bet money that you were going to stay and become a star."

"It didn't suit me." I hesitated, and then looked into his eyes. "And there were some things about New Jersey that I missed."

"I missed you also," he said, "but we need to talk about that."

"I know. Let's talk."

We sat down on a big boulder, swinging our legs off so that our heels tapped every once in a while. We were both wearing jeans and sweaters — his brown and mine green. The trees above us were maples and oaks; from their thick trunks I judged them to be hundreds of years old. Their branches made a latticed roof overhead, while their roots sank deep into the forest floor. The rock was covered with patches of moss and lichen. Vines dangled down from high branches. It felt like a very real, old, and solid place.

"I told you about Annie in my letter."

"The girl you met at the shore."

"I never thought you'd come back. I was sure you'd find some handsome guy out in Los Angeles. . . ."

"I did for a little while."

Our heels clicked back against the rock. Tap. Tap.

"This is confusing to me," Eric said. "I like you and I like her." He took a deep breath and his body shivered. "I guess for a little while I need to go out with her, and just be friends with you. See where it leads." He hesitated — it was as if he was afraid he was hurting me by speaking his mind.

I took his hand, and our fingers folded together. "Go on," I whispered.

"I don't blame you for anything. I know you had to do what you did. But I kind of feel like you went away from me for two months, by your own choice, and Annie was there for me all summer. I can't go out with two people at once. I still don't know her very well and I don't know what it will be like trying to go out with someone from twenty miles away. She doesn't even live in Bergen County. But I guess I owe it to her to try. . . ."

"If that's how you feel, then that's what you should do."

"Maybe I've screwed things up," he said. "I'm sorry, Liz. I'm not very smart about relationships. If I've hurt you, I'm really sorry."

I kissed him on the cheek and then actually laughed out loud.

He looked at me like I was crazy. "Why are you kissing me and laughing when I know I'm hurting you?"

I ran my fingers through his unruly mop of hair and put my head lightly against his shoulder. "Yes, I'm disappointed. I wanted to come home and have it be like it was before. But, Eric . . ." I put my lips next to his ear and whispered, "don't you ever, ever, ever apologize to me for telling me the truth. You don't know how reassuring it feels. Even if what you're saying is painful." And I kissed him again, on the ear.

He put his arm around me. His green wool sweater felt warm and comfortingly scratchy against my cheek. "Okay," he whispered. And we sat there together in silence, side by side, watching the river flow slowly through the cool autumn afternoon.